The HUNTER'S MOON

THE
HUNTER'S MOON

BOOK ONE IN
THE CHRONICLES OF FAERIE

O.R. MELLING

PUFFIN BOOKS

PUFFIN BOOKS

Published by the Penguin Group

Penguin Books Canada Ltd, 10 Alcorn Avenue, Toronto, Ontario, Canada M4V 3B2

Penguin Books Ltd, 27 Wrights Lane, London W8 5TZ, England

Penguin Putnam Inc., 375 Hudson Street, New York, New York 10014, U.S.A.

Penguin Books Australia Ltd, Ringwood, Victoria, Australia

Penguin Books (NZ) Ltd, cnr Rosedale and Airborne Roads, Albany,
Auckland 1310, New Zealand

Penguin Books Ltd, Registered Offices: Harmondsworth, Middlesex, England

First published by HarperCollins Publishers Ltd, 1993

Published in Puffin Books, 2000

1 3 5 7 9 10 8 6 4 2

Copyright © O.R. Melling, 1993

*Publisher's note: This book is a work of fiction. Names, characters, places and incidents
either are the product of the author's imagination or are used fictitiously, and any
resemblance to actual persons living or dead, events, or locales is entirely coincidental.*

Author representation: Transatlantic Literary Agency Inc.,
72 Glengowan Road, Toronto, Ontario M4N 1G4

Manufactured in Canada

CANADIAN CATALOGUING IN PUBLICATION DATA

Melling, O.R.
The hunter's moon

(The chronicles of Faerie ; 1)
ISBN 0-14-130991-1

I. Title.   II Series: Melling, O.R. Chronicles of Faerie ; 1.

PS8576.E463H86 2000   jC813'.54   C00-930619-6
PZ7.M51625Hu 2000

Visit Penguin Canada's web site at **www.penguin.ca**

Traveller, these stories are for you,
to help you on your way.

O.R.

ACKNOWLEDGEMENTS

THE QUOTATION ON PAGE 31 is from Lady Wilde's *Ancient Legends of Ireland* first published in 1888 and reprinted 1971 by O'Gorman Ltd., Galway, Ireland, used here with the kind permission of the publisher.

The Weird of Fionavar is a rare book of poems by Ella Young, published by the Talbot Press, Dublin 1922 (no longer extant).

Thank you to The Canada Council for the Arts for grant support, 1992.

Heartfelt thanks to the following: my own Findabhair of the laughing fairies; Meg Masters, former editor, who inspired this series; Barbara Berson, new editor, who is overseeing its birth; my wonderful agents Lynn and David Bennett of Transatlantic Inc; the Hamu Famu in Toronto; Breege McCrory of Inch Island who told me fairy tales and showed me Dunfinn; the Arbuckle-Brady clan of Meitheal Fort and L'Derry; Frank and Eve of Burrin, Clare; Georgie

Whelan, my mainstay with Finn; Deirdre and Yvonne Whelan, sisters and dancing fools in TO; *Na Daoine Maithe*, for their generous permission and assistance.

Come away, O human child!
To the waters and the wild
With a faery, hand in hand,
For the world's more full of weeping
than you can understand.

"The Stolen Child"
W. B. Yeats

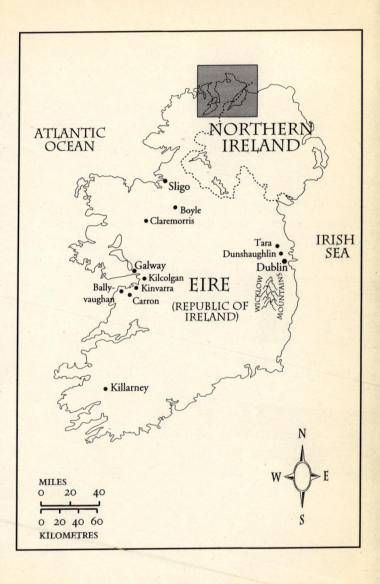

THE

HUNTER'S MOON

BOOK ONE IN
THE CHRONICLES OF FAERIE

CHAPTER ONE

The muddy waters of the River Liffey flowed sluggishly along the stone-walled quays. Like a weary old man in a dirty brown coat, it wended its way through the noise and grime of Dublin City.

"Have you forgotten how to sing?" murmured the dark-eyed young man who leaned over the railings of the Ha'penny Bridge. His sloe-black eyes went darker still as he brooded on the ancient river. "When we called you Rurthach you purled like a young stream. What have they done to you?"

A shudder passed through him as he regarded his surroundings: concrete towers, crowded streets, the blare of traffic. How could they live this way?

He was about to leave, eager to complete his mission and be gone from there, when he took pity on the river. A ray of gold flashed from his fingers to strike the turbid waters like a shaft of light. It was only for a second, the blink of an eye, but in that moment the river ran free. The young man was already hurrying away from the bridge as the clear rushing waters sang their brief song. *The King passed by. Long live the King.*

When he came to a second-hand bookshop and café, he hesitated outside. Human meeting places made him uneasy. It was an old building, of worn red brick, with high arched windows that overlooked the river. Inside was the scent of books. The musty solitude was reminiscent of a quiet forest glade. Winding wooden stairs brought him to the third floor and there she was, as he knew she would be, seated at a table by the window. She was reading a letter. Lit up by sunlight, the golden-brown hair fell over her face like a veil. A young girl, almost a woman, she was dressed in the fashion of urban youth: black sweater, black skirt, black stockings and shoes. Her slender shoulders shook with laughter as she read.

> Dear Findabhair,
>
> Gawd, your name is impossible to spell. I have to look at it twice every time I write it. You're a witch for not letting me call you Finn any more. But hey, forget the complaints—I'm coming over at last! Mom and Dad are forking out the fare (I'm not proud) and I've saved every cent for our trip. YAHOO.
>
> You still want to travel around, don't you?

You haven't changed your mind? Don't fall in love with anyone before I get there or something stupid like that. I don't want any third parties tagging along.

Ignore that last part—I'm just feeling insecure. Can't wait to see you. I'm packing already. Tell Aunt Pat to get in some skim milk—I'm on a diet again. (It's a losing battle. Wait till you see me—I'm a real porker.) And *no hairy bacon*, please!

See you soon,
Lots of love,
Your Canuck of a cuz,
Gwen
xxx

"May I sit down?"

Findabhair was about to point out archly that there were plenty of empty tables, when she looked up. The words died in her throat. He was exactly her idea of a stunning young man: sharp elegant features like a hawk's, hair black as the night and keen dark eyes. Like her, he favoured black, and she admired the quirkiness of the silk jacket with tight jeans. He seemed somehow familiar, but she couldn't think where she might have seen him before.

"Do I know you?"

"Not yet. You're remembering the future. That's possible, you know. Déjà vu."

It was a fascinating idea as well as a good line. Findabhair beamed a smile as he sat down beside her.

"This is a gift I wish to give you."

Her eyes widened as they settled on the little volume. Gold lettering on green leather. *The Weird of Fionavar.*

"That's my name! Well, a version of it. I prefer the Old Irish spelling and I pronounce it 'finn-ah-veer,' but it's the same name. What a brilliant coincidence! How did you—"

"There's no time," he said.

An urgency had crept into his voice, which made her look around for some secret danger. He turned the pages in front of her. Crisp and browned with age, each leaf contained a poem.

"Read this one, please."

Enjoying the odd encounter, Findabhair didn't stop to question him but read out loud.

"Folk of the *Sídhe*-Mound under the hill,
I hear their music when the wind is still.
Fionavar, Fionavar
You need not fear for pain or woe,
Fionavar, the road you go."

"Do you know what a *Sídhe*-Mound is?" he asked her.

"Of course," she said. "I love Celtic myths and tales. It's a fairy hill."

"Will you meet me there?"

He stood up, obviously about to leave.

"Where? Where will I meet you?" Findabhair's voice sounded desperate. She was surprised at herself, but she didn't want him to go.

He leaned toward her, and she thought he was going to kiss her. Instead he brushed his lips against her ear. "Tara," he whispered. "Come to Tara."

And then he was gone.

A strange sadness settled over her. Something wonderful had happened and she had lost it already.

Findabhair put her hand to her eyes. She looked around her in confusion. What was she doing? She glanced out the window to where the River Liffey flowed past. A slight dark figure stood on the Ha'penny Bridge before disappearing into the busy crowds. He meant nothing to her. She turned back to her cousin's letter but realized she had finished reading it.

"Lost in a daydream," she muttered to herself. "I only wish I could remember it."

Then she spotted the little book on the table. Surprised to see her own name in the title, she opened it thoughtfully and began reading the poems. They were lovely. The kind she liked. Though she hadn't intended to buy anything, she brought it up to the counter.

"How much is this?"

The red-haired man looked at the book and shook his head. "It's not ours. Didn't you bring it in with you? I remember noticing it when I took your coffee over. A nice antique."

"I guess it is mine." She laughed with embarrassment. "Sorry, I'm feeling a bit off today."

"You too?" The bookseller grinned. "Do you know, I've had two customers tell me they saw the Liffey bloomin' clean for a minute. What do you make of that?"

"Too much sun."

"That's what it is. And we're going to have a grand summer by the looks of it."

"Yes, I think we will," Findabhair agreed softly.

She tucked the book into her handbag and left the shop.

Chapter Two

Gwen Woods stood in the doorway of her cousin's bedroom. It was like peering into Aladdin's cave. The light was dim since the curtains were still drawn, and the room seemed to dance with colour and shadow. Vivid cloths and gauzy veils were draped across the walls and ceiling. Shelves of books shared space with shining brass objects, glass figurines, and woven baskets strung on ribbons. Seashell chimes and tubular bells dangled musically at the window. Posters of Enya and Clannad hung alongside prints of dream landscapes and other worlds. Gwen had to grin. The clutter of curios, books and fantasy was like her own room in Toronto.

"Finn? I mean, Findabhair?" she called into the gloom. "It's me. Gwen. I'm here."

At first there was no response from the big bed in the corner. Then came a grumble followed by a moan and suddenly the blankets flew into the air.

"What's this?" cried Findabhair as she jumped out of bed. "What am I doing here? I should be at the airport meeting you!"

The two girls hugged wildly as they laughed and talked and exclaimed over each other's appearance. Four years had passed since they were last together, and both were now sixteen.

"Your dad said he gave up after the tenth call. I've unpacked and everything."

Findabhair looked ashamed for almost a minute, then hurried to get dressed.

Though they were first cousins, there was little resemblance between the girls except for the golden-brown colour of their hair. Whereas Findabhair was tall and slender with thick wavy hair that fell to her shoulders, Gwen was small and plump with a head of closely cropped curls.

"You look fantastic," Gwen said enviously. She flung herself on the bed. "And here's me. Blimp City."

Findabhair frowned as she pulled on black leggings, black T-shirt and heavy black boots. "Everyone in America wants to be skinny, don't they? It's daft. You shouldn't knock yourself so much. You look brilliant."

"Thanks." Gwen grinned at her cousin, who was now fully dressed. "Do you work in a funeral parlour or what?"

Findabhair scrutinized Gwen's blue jeans, running

shoes and loud pink blouse. "Does that shirt come with a battery?"

"I promised my mom we wouldn't fight."

"Me too."

They snickered.

It was so easy to slip back into their old banter. They had been best friends since they could walk and talk. Their mothers were sisters and very close. After the older one emigrated to Canada, where she married and settled down, each brought her children across the ocean to meet on holidays. The two girls would write to keep up their friendship.

"Did you see the Robin Hood movie?" Gwen asked.

She was rummaging through books and the audio-tape collection while Findabhair put on her make-up.

"Yes. I liked it, but not as much as the television series. They're more magical."

"Yeah, I think so too. Great song from Bryan Adams though."

"That was the best part. He's not bad for an American."

"Canadian!" Gwen protested, then she realized Findabhair was teasing.

Gwen moved to the window to gaze out at the Irish Sea. The sun glimmered on rolling green waves that dashed to the shore like white horses. She loved this old house that overlooked the sea front, with the Wicklow Mountains rising up beyond. So many childhood summers belonged to this place. So many secret hopes and dreams.

"Right, I'm human," Findabhair declared.

She gazed at her image in the mirror to admire the contrast of bright red lipstick, black eyeliner and a light dusting of white face powder.

It was Gwen's turn to frown. "You haven't become an airhead on me, have you?"

"What do you mean!"

"You know. Only thinking about boys, make-up and clothes. Have you changed? Have you forgotten the important stuff?"

Findabhair looked thoughtful and a smile flickered over her features. "All our secret hopes and dreams?"

She said it softly. The phrase was a password between them, referring to their love of fantasy in any form—books, music, movies or art. Even the last time they met, though almost thirteen years old, they had resumed their search for a door or passageway that might lead to other worlds. Not finding that door, they had promised themselves a future quest in the wider world.

The two girls stared at each other now without speaking. Gwen's silhouette shone in the window, outlined by the light of the sky behind her. Findabhair was a double image, reflected in her looking glass like a shadowy Alice.

"Have I forgotten?!" she repeated. "But isn't that

why you're here? You weren't just planning to be a tourist, were you?"

"No, no. Of course not!" Gwen felt as if she might burst with happiness. Despite the differences, it seemed nothing had really changed after all. Gwen had been so careful in her letters, afraid that her cousin might think her childish. And here all along Findabhair had taken for granted what Gwen was nursing as a secret plan. They were setting out on their quest at last!

Findabhair spread out a map of Ireland on the floor.

"I've convinced Mum and Dad we can travel alone. After all, fourteen-year-olds go to the Gaeltacht to learn Irish. We just have to phone regularly to let them know where we are."

Gwen knelt beside Findabhair to view the map. The Thirty-Two Counties lay before her like a cloth of green and gold.

"We'll start at Tara," Findabhair said matter-of-factly, "since it's the ancient royal centre."

"Wait a minute. I thought we were ending the trip at Tara. That's what you agreed in your last letter. Saving the best for the last, like the Holy Grail or whatever."

"That wouldn't be right," Findabhair argued. "Everything begins at Tara. It's the seat of the High Kings and the sacred assembly place of the tribes of Ireland. Kings, Queens and Druids gathered there. Where else would you start a quest? It's the obvious place."

"Maybe to you," Gwen said angrily. "I just can't believe you've changed our plans without letting me know!"

A major fight seemed inevitable, with every possibility that the journey might end before it began. Findabhair sat back, uncertain and confused. There was something she wanted to tell Gwen if she could only remember. And why this insistence on Tara? Gwen was right, of course. It was unfair. And yet. And yet . . .

"Gwen, this will sound odd, I really can't explain it. But somehow I know we should go to Tara first."

Gwen was swayed by her cousin's sincerity. "Hey, okay! When you put it that way . . . It's following the true spirit of the quest. We must go on instinct. 'Seek and ye shall find.' "

Findabhair burst out laughing as she nodded enthusiastically. "We're hopeless romantics, you know."

"Hope*ful*," Gwen corrected her.

Chapter Three

The summer sun warmed the road that traversed the green Plain of Meath. Standing on the verge, Gwen and Findabhair faced the traffic with their thumbs out. Both shouldered heavy knapsacks topped with sleeping bags. While Findabhair's displayed the Irish tricolour flag, Gwen's sported the bright red maple leaf.

"I love being in the countryside," said Gwen, taking a deep breath of fresh air.

"We're on a bloody main road going nowhere rapidly," Findabhair grumbled.

She was annoyed that they were still standing in the same spot where they had been dropped off a half-hour earlier.

Gwen didn't mind how long she stood there, as long as it didn't rain. Though it was a busy road with cars speeding past like any Canadian highway, everything else was different. The view was one of limitless green, as if she were standing in the midst of a summer sea. The gentle roll of hills and fields, the lush green trees and hedgerows were a wonderful change from Toronto's tall buildings and grey-paved streets. Clouds drifted lazily in a shining blue sky. A warm haze hovered over the landscape like a dream.

"My mom would go crazy if she knew we were hitchhiking. It's a definite no-no where I come from. You can end up dead at the side of the road."

"God," said Findabhair with a shiver. "It's safe enough here. Everyone does it, especially in the country. But we won't get in if anyone looks suspicious. We're not that far away. I'm on for walking if no one stops in the next ten minutes."

The ten minutes were nearly up when a battered old car came into sight and slowed down as it approached them.

"What a dote!" cried Findabhair.

Though it had seen better days, the little Triumph Herald retained a dignity all its own. The rounded body and humped roof gave it a homely friendly look. The rusted chrome over the headlights were like bushy eyebrows. The forest-green paint was mottled and chipped like a freckled face. When the car stopped in front of them, one glance within assured the girls they were safe.

The driver suited his car. A wizened little man with a face like a dried apple, he had two bright beads for eyes which winked at them merrily. His suit was brown tweed, worn and patched in places, the jacket closed with a large safety pin. A peaked cap was perched on his head, the same dark-red colouring as his ruddy cheeks. He leaned forward to open the passenger door, and the girls flung their knapsacks into the back. Gwen hurried in with them, leaving the front seat to Findabhair, along with the job of talking to the driver.

"And where may I take you, my fine ladies?" asked the little man, craning his neck to look back at Gwen, then squinting at Findabhair as she banged the door shut.

"We're off to Tara," Findabhair said grandly, "to give our regards to the High King of Ireland."

"Teamhair na Ríogh it is," he said with a chuckle. "'Tis near enough, but far away for some."

The interior of the car was as dilapidated as its owner. Shabby blankets covered rips in the upholstery. The wooden dashboard was pockmarked with wormholes. Scattered over the floor and on the shelf in the back were heaps of old shoes and boots. Findabhair noted the moss that grew on the carpet at her feet. She wanted to turn around and grin at Gwen but felt it would be rude.

"Now what would ye be wanting at Tara?" the old man enquired. "Leprechauns and pots of gold, is it?"

His voice had a wheedling tone that made Gwen uneasy, but Findabhair was enjoying his eccentricity.

"What do we look like, a pair of gobs?" she retorted with spirit.

"Then ye wouldn't put any faith in the likes of the Good People?"

His persistence reached a higher note. In the back, Gwen heard some kind of warning in that quaver. Findabhair only snorted indignantly.

"If you mean wee things with wings and shoe-makers with pointy ears, no. That's a load of American rubbish and an insult to our cultural heritage."

While Findabhair warmed to her subject, exhorting on the commercial abuse of Irish mythology, Gwen was noticing the plethora of footwear around her. Buckled shoes and ladies slippers, high heels and working boots, some with worn-out soles and holes in the toes, others with tongues hanging out and their laces missing. Not one had a visible match. She found herself wondering about the shape of the little man's ears hidden under his cap. Without thinking, she leaned forward to interrupt her cousin.

"We do believe in . . . something. The something that's in the ancient tales and poetry. That's why we're travelling. It's sort of a quest. To see if that something still exists."

A silence settled inside the car. Gwen's words seemed to hang in the air, glittering with meaning, as if they were more important than she intended them to be. She felt suddenly nervous.

"Ah now." The old man's cackle broke the mood.

"I wouldn't know what the likes of ye scholars would be on about."

He stopped the car.

"Out ye go, the pair of ye."

The dismissal was curt, and they sat stunned for a minute; then they saw the signpost on the road in front of them.

TEAMHAIR. TARA.

"Up that boreen ye go, and what you're looking for will find ye."

"Ta for the lift," said Findabhair.

"Have a nice day," added Gwen.

They walked up the narrow lane, shifting the weight of the knapsacks on their backs. The way was lined with overhanging trees and bushes laden with white blossoms like brides. Bees hummed in the warm greenery. It was like a leafy hall with an arched roof of branches, leading them to a palace.

"Did he give you the creeps?" asked Gwen, as they stepped aside to let a tour bus crawl past.

"What? Not at all. He was good crack. Odd as two left feet. I just don't like all that shamrocks-and-leprechauns stuff. He was treating us like tourists."

"I don't think so," Gwen said. "He was testing us in some way, trying to find out something. And I think he succeeded. I should have kept my big yap shut."

"I wouldn't worry about it. I'm sure he hadn't a bog what you were on about. Daft as a brush."

Gwen was not reassured. In fact, she suspected the

opposite was true. Though she couldn't explain how or why, something told her the little man understood her words more than she did. The uneasy feeling would have continued to nag her, but Tara itself presented a sudden distraction.

CHAPTER FOUR

"Hurrah! a res-
taurant. I'm starving," said Gwen.

The road had brought them to a cluster of buildings including a public lavatory, a souvenir shop and a
tea room. Wooden tables and chairs stood outside in
the sunshine inviting them to sit down. To their right
was a car park, and beyond it, the iron gates that led
onto the Hill of Tara.

"You told me to keep you away from food."

"I meant soda bread and sausages and stuff like
that. Something small will do. All this fresh air makes
me hungry."

"First we see Tara, then we eat," Findabhair
insisted, dragging Gwen away.

"You're as bossy as ever."

To the unknowing eye, Tara is simply a rambling
area of grassy mounds and trenches. The man-made

earthworks are all that remain of a royal centre abandoned fourteen centuries ago. And to the unknowing
eye, Tara holds no other charm than the magnificent
view of the countryside, which unfolds from its height.
But to Gwen and Findabhair it meant much more.

Bright-surfaced Teamhair, the poets called her. Tara of
the Kings. The glory of this place was subtle and
secret. It lingered in the shadows of the long grass,
whispered on the wind. *Teach Míodchuarta.* The Banquet Hall. Once it was a house of fourteen doors:
seven to face the golden sun and seven to face the
silver moon. *Rath na Ríogh.* The Royal Enclosure. This
great circle was a kingly fort crowned long ago with a
palisade of oak.

The two girls left their knapsacks at the gate and
roamed freely over the earthworks. Ignoring the
tourists and the click of cameras, they wandered in a
happy daze. It was this very ground that the Druids
had trod. And the Kings and the Queens and the
Celtic warriors. They had gathered here for games and
festivals, for the making of laws and the calling up of
armies. And more mysteriously, on lunar feasts, for sac-
rificial rites and ritual burials.

Gwen climbed onto the Grave Mound of the
Hostages, a small hill like an upturned bowl. Around
her spread the landscape like a woven cloth. Fields of
yellow and green were patched with brown where the
soil had been ploughed. In the distance, a blue rim of
mountains etched a gentle outline against the breadth

of sky. The grass was warm, and Gwen lay down to watch the clouds. They were moving swiftly, herded like sheep by the wind. She felt lost and glad, caught up in the flow of forever.

Ever restless and active, Findabhair was still investigating the site like a hunter's hound. She arrived at the Mound of the Hostages from a different angle and discovered the opening in the hill barred by a padlocked gate.

"It's a cairn!" she called up to her cousin, who didn't answer.

Findabhair pressed her face against the gate and peered inside. Just as she thought. Though the mound appeared to be a grassy hill, it was man-made with heavy slabs of stone. The interior was hollow like a cave. Like a tomb. She shivered. The core was dim, but she could see that the great stone on her left was scored with circular designs. She wished she knew what they meant. A strange yearning came over her. She wanted to get in there.

On top of the mound, Gwen had lapsed into a daydream, unaware that her cousin was near. The clouds seemed to fall out of the sky, gently, slowly, to descend upon the hill. She was surrounded by mist, like a pale-grey sea, as if she were lying on the crest of a green island. Then her ears began to throb with a low humming sound. She felt her blood rise in response, the way feet itch to dance. Under the hum, or was it beyond, came the echo of music. It seemed to come from a great distance like the whisper in the whorl of a shell. There was a deep rumbling like far-off drums or thunder, but also high reedy notes like a silver flute. She strained to listen, but the throbbing interfered as if her ears were not attuned to such sounds.

Below her, Findabhair leaned against the gate, eyes half-closed. She too was wrapped in a milky stillness, listening to the eerie music. Then another sound reached her. The fierce gallop of a horse. As the hooves drew near, a voice called out from the mist.

I shall take my Beloved from the Mound of the Hostages.

On the hilltop, Gwen was suddenly awake. Storm clouds had covered the sun like the dark swirl of a cape. The grass was cold against her back. She scrambled to her feet. "Where are you?" she cried out.

Findabhair jumped back from the gate as if it had burned her. Bewildered, she looked up at Gwen, who was staring wildly down.

Without a word, the two ran from the grave mound, grabbed their knapsacks and hurried to the tea room. Only when they were safely inside, surrounded by people, did they meet each other's eyes. With cups of tea and buttered scones in front of them, they were able to acknowledge the truth.

"It's here," Gwen whispered.

"It still exists." Findabhair nodded.

They grinned at each other, barely able to contain the huge nameless excitement that was rising within them.

"I feel like standing on the table and roaring it out at the top of my lungs," Findabhair said, lowering her voice so she wouldn't give in to the temptation.

"I know what you mean. I could run up a mountain or leap off a cliff!"

Gwen slurped her tea loudly, which sent the two of them into a fit of giggles. Both felt light-headed and giddy.

"Can you remember what happened?"

Findabhair frowned with the effort to concentrate, but it was too like a dream. The kind that hints with vague images but can't be recalled. She shook her head.

"Me neither," Gwen sighed. "It's gone. But there was something. It felt like . . . an invitation?"

"Yes! Exactly. So how do we accept?"

Gwen had sudden misgivings. "Should we? Weren't you afraid?"

"Of course I was." Findabhair snorted. "The unknown would scare the bejesus out of anyone. But you wouldn't let that stop you, would you?"

"I suppose not," Gwen said. She wasn't as headstrong as her cousin, but she wasn't about to be left behind either.

"We'll camp overnight in the mound," Findabhair declared.

"Omigod!" wailed Gwen.

The couple at the next table looked over at them, but Findabhair continued inexorably. "I've always wanted to sleep in a mound or on top of a fairy rath. You know that's how it's done according to all the legends and vision-poems."

She closed her eyes for a moment as she almost remembered something. It had to do with a *Sídhe*-Mound and Tara as well. Something in a book? The memory eluded her, and yet whatever it was left her with the certainty of what she wanted to do. But if Gwen refused?

Despite a self-admitted cowardice, Gwen was already considering the proposition. It was no accident that she was here with her cousin facing this decision. While it wasn't exactly what she had in mind, it was the kind of adventure that suited a quest. Wasn't this why she had come to Ireland? Though a hundred doubts and fears assailed her, some queenly part was giving the royal nod.

"You realize we'll be breaking the law," she pointed out. "Trespassing and who knows what else."

"Forced entry," Findabhair said. "There's a padlock on the gate to the mound. If we get nicked, you can do the talking. When they hear the American accent, they'll let us off."

Findabhair was jubilant. She knew Gwen had agreed to do it since she was working on the details.

"Canadian accent," Gwen said, with a glint in her eye. "And we won't get caught."

CHAPTER FIVE

[decorative band]

It was nearly midnight when the girls returned to Tara. They had passed the time in the village of Dunshaughlin, then walked back for the sake of safety and secrecy. With furtive step they hurried past the tea room, now closed and dark. A quick scramble over the low stone wall and they were on the Hill of Tara.

In the silence of the night, it was a desolate place. Abandoned to shadows, empty of life. The mounds and ridges lay like fallen tombstones in the dark wet grass. A cold wind whistled eerily. They had to fight off the sense that they were treading on forbidden ground.

"Hold the torch over my shoulder," Findabhair whispered, as she crouched in front of the Mound of the Hostages.

The mound seemed to brood over them. Gwen kept looking behind her as she trained the flashlight on the gate that barred their way.

Gently, Findabhair worked the padlock with her penknife. For a while the only sound to be heard was the quick rasp of their breath and the scraping of the knife. Then came a triumphant click.

"We're in," she said.

They were too excited for last-minute doubts, too busy making themselves comfortable in the cramped inner space. It was like a cave, cold and damp, and they had to stoop as they moved about. They spread out the groundsheet and unrolled their sleeping bags.

"We should lie with our heads to this," Findabhair suggested, playing the light over the great stone engraved with designs.

"That's what the Druids probably did," Gwen agreed. "And I think we should stay dressed."

"For a quick escape?"

"You never know."

The flashlight shone inside the mound like a little campfire, casting their shadows over the walls and roof. But once they were settled inside their sleeping bags, they turned it off. The darkness engulfed them. Neither could speak at first, overwhelmed by what they had done. The heavy scent of stone and earth was unmistakable. They were enclosed in a tomb. Slowly their eyes grew accustomed to the dimness and they breathed more easily.

"What do you think might happen?" Gwen whispered.

"Anything. Nothing," Findabhair answered seri-ously. "I'm not sure I really care. Just to do this is an adventure in itself."

"I know what you mean. I wouldn't have done it on my own in a million years, but I love it. I'm really glad we're here."

"Me too," Findabhair said with a low laugh. "Anyone else would think we were mad."

"Guess what? I meant to tell you earlier. I was looking at the guidebook to Tara when we were in the store and there's a place nearby called Tobar Finn. What do you make of that?"

Findabhair shivered with excitement. "*Tobar*'s the Old Irish word for 'well,' but what a brilliant coinci-dence that it's named after me. I knew it was my des-tiny to come here!"

"Mine too," Gwen pointed out. "My name's the same as yours. Finn and Gwen. Findabhair and Gwen-hyvar. I've got the Welsh and you've got the Irish, but it's the same name."

"Of course," her cousin murmured.

It's the same name. Why did that phrase sound familiar? With a start, Findabhair turned on the flash-light and began rummaging through her knapsack.

"What's up?" said Gwen.

"I can't believe I forgot to show you this. All the fuss of your arrival and getting ready for our trip put it out of my head. Here, look!"

Gwen turned sideways in her sleeping bag to

admire the little green book.

"*The Weird of Fionavar*," she said softly. The words seemed to whisper throughout the mound. "*Weird* means 'destiny,' doesn't it?"

She perused the pages and began to read out loud.

"Folk of the *Sídhe*-Mound under the hill,
   I hear their music when the wind is still.
   Fionavar, Fionavar—"

"Stop it!" Findabhair hissed. Though she didn't know why, she was suddenly overcome with a sense of foreboding. "What made you pick that one?"

Gwen caught the panic in her voice and felt a tremor of the same fear. "What's wrong?"

"I . . . I don't know." Findabhair took back the book and buried it quickly under the clothes in her knapsack. "Gwen. Was it my idea alone to come to Tara? Did I force you?"

"Don't be crazy. I planned to come here, too. Just not so soon."

"Then it could be me or it could be you or it could be both of us."

"Are you going to let me in on this train of thought or do I have to buy a ticket?"

Findabhair grinned sheepishly. "Sorry. I'll let you know as soon as I do. I think I had a dream about that book and now I'm getting premonitions."

"Listen, kiddo, this is not the time and place. You're

going to spook us out. Let's leave it till the morning, okay?"

"You're right." Findabhair laughed. "Change the subject."

She turned off the flashlight. They continued to talk in low tones, making plans for the next stage of their journey. Though neither said it to the other, each was haunted by a strange uneasiness, and they kept talking to ignore their fears. But eventually their conversation was punctuated by sighs and yawns till both dropped off to sleep.

Fast asleep, neither sensed the change that was occurring outside the mound.

As darkness met light in the dim borderland before dawn, the stillness over Tara began to shudder. To come alive. Before time could cross from night to day, one world was about to eclipse another.

The empty mounds and earthworks began to glow as if a falling star had landed. From the jagged contours of the hills and ridges rose the shining silhouette of a palace hall. Walls of gold and silver glittered with gems. A thousand candles blazed within. From the high graceful windows, sweet sounds issued forth: unearthly music, murmur and laughter.

Padded footfalls came out of the shadows. Voices whispered on the wind.

"There are humans in the mound!"

"Does the King know of this?"

A wild laugh trilled like a panpipe.

"Do you not know? Before this night is through, he will have taken a bride!"

At that very moment Gwen turned in her sleep, troubled by a hint of warning. Beside her, Findabhair did the same. Their heads now rested at the centre of the great stone. Light seeped into the grooves of the circular designs till they shone like halos behind the girls.

"Gwenhyvar. Fair one. Gwenhyvar fair," a voice called inside the mound.

Gwen frowned in her sleep. Behind her eyelids, motes of dusty light joined together to form an image at the foot of her sleeping bag. A youth of her own age, slender and naked. His skin glowed palely within the dark cave. Around his neck were beads of bronze and amber.

"You must leave this place, Gwenhyvar. Danger draws near. Be quick!"

Though convinced she was dreaming, Gwen knew somehow that the urgency was real. She wrestled with the bonds of sleep in vain. Each effort to wake sent her tumbling dizzily through wild dimensions of colour and space.

"Help me!" she cried to the boy.

"I cannot," he said sadly, as he faded away. "I am only a barrow wight. The shadow of my self long gone. I died in this place many centuries ago. I have no power other than to warn you."

Despite her growing fear, Gwen felt a pang of

sorrow for him. What terrible thing had happened to hold his spirit to this mound?

While Gwen struggled against the powers of sleep, Findabhair was dancing her way through a seductive fantasy. She was at a fancy-dress ball. Everyone was in splendid costume with masks parading peacock plumes. A gown of many colours clung to her body. Her hair was bound up in jewelled combs. Twirling and swirling to a breathtaking waltz, she danced in the arms of a startling young man. As is the way of dreams, he was somehow familiar though she didn't know his name nor had she any memory of him. His features were sharp like a hawk's, with piercing dark eyes. The lips were as red as berries, the hair midnight black. He didn't appear to be speaking, but his words spun in her mind in time to the music.

O lady, if thou comest to my proud people,
'Tis a golden crown shall circle thy head,
Thou shalt dwell by the sweet streams of
    my country,
And drink mead and wine in the arms of
    thy lover.

His arms tightened around her waist. "Come with me," he said, and it was more a command than a request.

There was no beginning to the dream, so Findabhair didn't consider a possible end. In that moment there was only the dance and the music and her dark-eyed partner. There was no other likely answer.

Yes.

The word hissed on Findabhair's lips as she lay sleeping. Beside her, Gwen turned restlessly again, sensing the doom that was upon them.

The echo of hooves. Galloping toward them. Louder and louder as the horse drew near. The gate of the mound burst open!

The inner core was now immense, a cathedral of dark stone. In charged a stallion, black as the night, with nostrils flared and snorting flame. Astride the horse was a dark-caped rider with a face like a hawk's. He leaned down from his saddle to scoop up his prey.

"No!" cried Gwen.

The horse reared and pawed the air. The rider stared down. There was no remorse or pity in those sloe-black eyes.

"No is your answer, but yes was hers. I have taken my bride from the Mound of the Hostages!"

With Findabhair slung over his saddle, sleeping bag and all, he rode out of the mound.

"No!" Gwen screamed once more, loud enough to wake herself at last.

Shaking with terror she turned to her cousin for comfort from her nightmare. New terror gorged her throat.

Findabhair was gone.

CHAPTER SIX

GWEN COULDN'T accept what her eyes were telling her. Though Findabhair and everything belonging to her had vanished, there had to be a rational explanation. Her cousin had woken early and gone for a walk. She was playing a joke on Gwen. She was in the tea room having breakfast.

Gwen pulled on her boots and raced out of the mound.

It was a grey damp morning with a cloudy sky. The last trails of mist snaked through the dewy grass. As if to outrun her fears, she rushed from the hill and through the car park. The tea room was shut. Curtains were drawn over the windows like lidded eyes. Back to the mound to race over the earthworks, calling out Findabhair's name. Gwen's voice echoed through the stillness like a lonely wind. No response. No Findabhair. She stood quiet at last as the truth struck home.

Her cousin was gone. She had been abducted. But by whom? Or what?

Gwen shivered in the cool air as she fought back her tears. Slowly she recalled the night's dreams and visitations, confirming what she didn't want to admit. It was all very well to set out on a quest for things unimaginable, fantastical and unknown. It was quite a different matter to encounter them. Only now did Gwen realize that she hadn't really believed in the existence of another world. It had all been in the realm of the imagination. Till now.

"She's been stolen by the fairies."

The words issued from her mouth like mist on her breath, quivering with incredulity.

"What am I going to do?" she wailed.

Like a lost soul, she wandered again around Tara, reluctant to leave the place where she had last seen Findabhair. Still dazed, she returned to the mound and packed up her things. When she replaced the padlock on the gate, she flinched as it clicked shut with an air of finality. Yet she knew that her cousin would not be found there. The rider had taken her from the mound. But to where?

Gwen trudged down the road, crying openly now, for her cousin who was gone and for herself left alone. Was Findabhair all right? How could Gwen help her? What should she do? Call her aunt and uncle? Contact the police? A kidnapping had occurred. In spite of her distress, Gwen's mouth twitched with humour as she imagined telling some stolid straight-faced sergeant that her cousin had been spirited away by the fairies. That picture cheered her up and set her thinking.

She would have to rescue Findabhair from the clutches of the fairies. What did she know about them? Behind the tales told to modern children was an old peasant belief in another race who lived alongside humans. They were called the "Good People" in an effort to appease them. Some said they were gods and others said they were fallen angels, not good enough for heaven but not bad enough for hell. Descriptions varied in all the books and stories. They could be tiny and winged like butterflies, or taller than mortals, shadowy beings of light and air. They didn't dislike humans, but then again they often played tricks on them, sometimes cruel ones. They were wilful and capricious and wild as the wind, loved music and dancing and perpetual frolic. Their favourite haunts were hills and forests, but they also dwelled inside mountains and in the ruins of ancient monuments.

This isn't getting me anywhere, Gwen thought, discouraged.

She was already missing Findabhair. Needing her. Gwen was the best thinker and the practical one, but Findabhair was more daring and decisive. She could act instinctively under any circumstances. She would know what to do.

"It's not fair," Gwen muttered bitterly. "I'm half a team and the game's already under way!"

When she came to the main road, she stopped in surprise. There in front of her, as if waiting patiently, was the battered old car. It shone with a new coat of green paint, but inside was the same wizened little man. He beckoned to her.

After all that had happened, Gwen knew without a doubt what she had only suspected the day before. She flung her knapsack into the back of the car and plumped down in the front seat to confront the leprechaun.

"Now don't be leppin' on me as if I'm to blame," he said quickly, when he saw the look on her face. "Fair's fair. Ye got what ye came for and I'm here to help."

With a crunch of gears, he shifted the car into traffic. Perched on two telephone books, white and yellow pages, he was like a child at the wheel as he peered over the dashboard.

"I'll get ye to Busaras with enough time for a bite to eat. Your bus leaves at nine o'clock sharp."

"And where am I going, if that's not too much to ask?" Gwen said archly.

At the same time she was feeling a huge sense of relief. All was not lost. The cavalry had arrived. And behind her relief was the rising thrill of excitement. Was this an adventure or what!

As if he could read her mind, the leprechaun chuckled. "Ye were looking for something and now it's found ye. Make the most of it. The fairy court is on its

summer circuit of the country. Ye'll have to be quick-
witted and light-footed if ye want to find your kin."

"Is she all right?"

"Right in the head? Is that what ye mean?"

"Is she safe?" Gwen persisted, annoyed with his
antics.

"That's a quare word. Is she safe and sound, are ye
askin' me?" His cackling laugh made Gwen uneasy.
"Sound in the head and safe in her bed. Have ye any
right to demand that after barging into secret places
without so much as a by-your-leave? If it's safety and
soundness ye wanted, ye'd have been better off follyin'
the Yankee trail to Killarney and all that blarney.
There's only one thing the fairy folk ask of your kind
and that's to be left alone. Ye broke more laws than
your own when ye slept in the mound."

Gwen shifted uncomfortably at his tirade. The leprechaun had gone red in the face, stealing the right-
eous indignation that had allowed her to be so bold.

"We didn't know," she said weakly.

"Ye did too," he retorted.

He was relentless. Gwen slumped in her seat. She
knew Findabhair wouldn't have let him browbeat her
into silence, but then she wasn't Findabhair. She
looked out the window at the countryside as it sped
past. Fields, farms, villages and towns were a multi-
coloured blur. The car was going amazingly fast for
something so old. As if it had wings.

"Okay. We did know what we were doing. Sort of.

And I guess we'll have to take the consequences. What happens next?"

"That's the spirit," said the leprechaun in a friendlier tone. "We all love a game and ye are two fine girls, strong and true. We'll get great sport out of ye."

Hardly a comforting thought but Gwen had already resigned herself to the situation.

They were now approaching Dublin City, and again Gwen was astonished by the speed of the old car. As the wide green lawns of the Phoenix Park flowed alongside them, the leprechaun suddenly doffed his cap with a jaunty wave.

"Your store of happiness to ye, *Mná na hEireann!*" he called, as they passed the palatial home of the President.

Gwen caught a glimpse of the pointy ears before the cap was clapped back on his head.

"A grand lady she is, our Mary Robinson," the leprechaun said fulsomely. "She believes in us, ye know, as do all truehearts, not like the rest of them blackguard politicians."

The car shot out of the park like a bullet and into the early morning traffic of the city. Pedestrian lights seemed to be irrelevant to the leprechaun as he dashed through intersections, scattering the crowds.

"You'd make a good cabby in New York," Gwen commented, gripping her seat.

"Heh? What's that?" But all his attention was on the road as he switched lanes with abandon.

They flew down the quays, the River Liffey a brown streak, and around the circle of the Customs House in a death-defying race with a tanker. Then swerving past a double-decker bus painted like a box of Smarties, they halted, brakes screeching, in front of the bus depot.

Gwen breathed a deep sigh of relief.

"Here ye are. Go west, young woman. Galway, I would suggest. Make your way to the Burren in the County of Clare. There'll be a banquet tonight at twilight. Carron is the nearest human habitation. Use your wits and ye'll find it."

He hauled out her knapsack and leaned it against the glass doors of the station. Gwen didn't want to get out of the car. Though she couldn't admit to liking the leprechaun, he was her only link to Findabhair and the fairies.

"Couldn't you drive me there?" she pleaded with him. "I'll pay for the gas, for your time . . . "

"Sure what would I want with the paper stuff ye use? Isn't it always becoming less with that deflation business?"

He held the door open to hurry her out, then his eyes shifted with a greedy gleam. "Have ye any gold on ye?"

"No," she said forlornly.

"Out ye go, then. I've done me job. I was to point ye in the general direction and that's what I've done. Good day to ye."

As he climbed back behind the wheel and turned the key in the ignition, Gwen ran to his window in a final attempt.

"Please," she begged.

The leprechaun hesitated. There was just the merest hint of sympathy in his eyes. He cocked his head and gave her a straight look.

"Ye've me heart scalded with your moaning, but I'll say this for ye. You've pluck for a foreigner. There wasn't a squeak out of ye about the driving. I'll give ye a word of wisdom. If you're betwixt and between, trust the one with red hair. Now that's more than I should be telling ye. I'm off. I've shoes to mend."

The Triumph Herald drove away, carrying with it her last hope of a direct route to the fairies. Disheartened, Gwen picked up her knapsack and walked into the bus station. After her recent experiences it was somewhat unsettling to be suddenly faced with the ordinary. There was a little cafeteria, a pub, a sweetshop and a ticket office. People sat on benches, reading newspapers and smoking cigarettes as they waited for their buses. Gwen felt disoriented, straddling two worlds, unsure of what was real.

The door of the cafeteria opened and the rich smell of bacon and eggs wafted toward her. The sign said FULL IRISH BREAKFAST, £3.50.

One of those and I'll be ready for anything, she told herself.

After all, there was a great mission before her,

places to go, people to meet, secrets to unearth. Boldly going . . .

"Touring the country?" the ticket man asked her with a friendly smile.

"Yeah, you could say that." Gwen smiled back.

ChAPTER SEVEN

LEAVING DUBLIN CITY
behind, the bus sped down the open road on its journey across Ireland. Cradled by the gentle rocking
motion, Gwen gazed peacefully out the window.

She had sent her worries on ahead to meet her at
her destination. For the next few hours she would just
sit back with nothing to do and no decisions to make.

A sudden shower poured from the heavens, pelt-
ing the landscape with sheets of rain. Through the
watery curtain, the countryside was a wash of green
and grey. Then the rain ceased as abruptly as it had
started, leaving everything breathless and silvered. Pud-
dles glistened at the side of the road. Hedges dripped
as if laden with dew. Gwen gasped with delight as a full
rainbow arched across the sky.

"A magical land," she murmured to herself.

Though the road took her through several large

towns, the dreamy feeling stayed with her. The sight of houses, meat-packing plants, dairies and railways only confirmed a notion that was growing inside her. There were two Irelands beyond her window, like two streams flowing side by side. One was a modern nation outfitted in concrete, electricity and machinery. The other was a timeless secret place that hinted continually of its presence. A tractor ploughed a field in the shadow of an ancient stone circle. Behind the flashy hotel were the ruins of a castle tower. High on a hilltop stood a grove of sacred oak. Like a magician playing with coloured scarves, the hidden land revealed itself in brief flashes and glimpses. But it was there, and Gwen knew she wasn't imagining it.

The bus arrived in Galway in the early afternoon. Gwen's panic returned as she stepped into the bustle of an unknown city. People hurried through the streets and around the square. Traffic moved slowly against the tide. Department store windows displayed their wares to lunchtime shoppers and groups of young people enjoying their holidays. She felt lost and lonely in that urban setting. All the faces in the crowd were strangers.

I wish Findabhair was here, she thought sadly.

Though she was getting hungry, Gwen decided not to delay in town. She had no idea how long it would take her to find the place the leprechaun had mentioned. She repeated his words since they were her only directions. *Make your way to the Burren in the*

County of Clare. There'll be a banquet tonight at twilight. Carron is the nearest human habitation.

A city bus brought her to the outskirts of Galway, where she found a spot to hitchhike. She didn't like thumbing alone, but she was too uncertain of where she was going to take public transportation. County Clare was south of Galway, according to her map, and that was all she knew.

When the sleek silver Mercedes drew up, Gwen hesitated anxiously. Inside sat a businessman in smart suit and tie, his briefcase on the floor beside him. The car interior was immaculate, pale blue leather and dark blue carpets. Country-and-Western music played on the tape deck. Gwen scrutinized the driver to judge his character. Fortysomething and slightly paunchy, he wore a gold wedding band on his left hand. His freckled face had an open friendly look. The deciding factor was the mop of red hair, brushed sideways in a half-hearted attempt to cover a bald patch. *If you're betwixt and between, trust the one with red hair.* He had already opened the passenger door.

"Your haversack can go in the back seat. There's plenty of room," he said, misinterpreting her slowness.

"Oh yeah. Thanks."

"How far are you going?" he asked, as the car eased back into traffic.

"The Burren. A place called Carron. It must be very small—it's not on my map."

"I know the spot. Near the University of Galway

Field Station. Are you a student? Is that where you're staying?"

"No. Yes. I mean, I could be. I don't know."

The businessman gave her a curious glance but continued in his friendly manner. "I can put you on the right road. My office is near Kilcolgan. You go west from there through Kinvarra to Ballyvaughan, then south to Carron. Anyone will tell you the way once you're in the Burren, though I wouldn't say your chance of a lift would be great. It's fairly barren country."

"I'll walk if I have to," Gwen said with a sigh.

He gave her another look, then frowned as he decided whether or not he should say anything.

"Is everything all right, pet?" he finally asked.

The kindness in his voice and the hint of a desire to help, broke down Gwen's defences. After all, he had the red hair that had been recommended to her and she so badly needed a friend. She told him about the night in Tara and how she had awoken to find her cousin gone. Then she explained that she was following the instructions of an odd little man. Though she avoided using the words "fairy" or "leprechaun," she knew it sounded crazy all the same. When she was finished, she wondered what she would do if he insisted on taking her to a hospital or police station.

After a long pause, the businessman spoke quietly. "Brave girls to sleep in a mound, but foolhardy too. There's no doubt about it. The fairies have got her."

Despite all that had happened, Gwen was stunned by his statement. "You believe in fairies?!"

He burst out laughing, a rich warm sound that was pleasant to hear. "Is it any less likely than believing in angels or saints or even Himself for that matter? I thought you looked a bit touched, but when I heard the American accent I was sure I was mistaken."

"Canadian," Gwen said. "Are you saying this kind of thing happens all the time?"

"Oh God no. But there was an old man in the village I was reared in who was taken by the fairies when he was young. To play a hurling match for them. He was the best hurler in the parish. He was never quite the same afterwards—had that look about him, not quite here, not quite there. I remember it after all these years, and when I saw you I was reminded of him."

Gwen shuddered. She was not at all happy with the idea of looking "touched."

"Have you eaten?" he asked, aware that she was upset. "We have a company café. Hot and cold buffet."

"That would be great." She felt better at the mention of food. "I'm Gwen Woods, by the way."

"Pleased to meet you, Gwen. Mattie O'Shea at your service."

They drove up the avenue of a company head office. Glass doors and wide windows gleamed in a façade of new brick. A rainbow of cars filled the parking lot.

"Not again!" Mattie swore as he spied the sheep grazing on the front lawn. A few had already made their way to the flower beds and were nosing amongst the roses. He parked the car and jumped out to chase off the culprits. After shooing them back into a nearby field, he used branches to block the gap where they had entered.

When Mattie returned to Gwen he was mopping his face with a handkerchief and puffing from his exertions. His hair was in wild disorder. She didn't know whether to laugh or sympathize.

"The grass is always greener in the next meadow." he said with a grin.

In gentlemanly fashion he held open the company door and ushered her down the corridor, nodding to the receptionist and other employees.

"What a lucky coincidence you picked me up," Gwen said, as he showed her into the cafeteria.

"No such thing as coincidence, pet" was Mattie's reply. "It was a very complicated set of events that made me so late for work today, including a mislaid report and a slow puncture, but I wouldn't hesitate to say that I was put in the right place at the right time to give you a hand. There are rules and traditions that govern the mingling of the fairy folk with our kind. They'll help you as much as hinder you. It's unfortunate, now, that we aren't near my home in Kerry. I could find you a fairy doctor. That's what they call the local wise man or wise woman who has 'the cure' for various ailments and who knows the ways of the Good People. Not too many of them left nowadays, but they still exist. Like the fairies themselves."

He let out one of his deep laughs. "I can tell you this. Pay attention to any voices you might hear out of the blue and don't think yourself mad. If you do cross over into Fairyland, take no food or drink or you'll come under their sway."

Mattie glanced at his watch. "God, I've a sales meeting in three minutes. Eat all around you—the food's free. I'll ask my secretary to drop you off on the road to Kinvarra. I'm sorry I can't be of more help to you, but here's my card. It has home and business numbers. Don't be afraid to telephone me if you're in trouble."

Overwhelmed by his kindness, Gwen reached up to give him a hug. "Thanks so much. You've been really great."

Mattie blushed furiously but looked pleased. "You'll have the whole place talking about me," he laughed, "Good luck to you."

He was halfway out the door when he hurried back to her with a serious look. "It just struck me. The fairy folk don't have as much power as they used to. There's not much room for them in a modern country. I don't understand how they could have taken your cousin. Is she Irish?"

"Yes. Both parents. My mother is Irish too, but she married a Canadian."

"That explains one thing," he said thoughtfully, "but not the other."

"What?" Gwen asked worriedly, catching his concern.

"I doubt they could have taken her if she didn't want to go."

Gwen caught her breath. Of course. The one point she hadn't considered, probably because she didn't want to face it. Findabhair may not have been "stolen" in the true sense of the word. And now Gwen realized something else she had hidden from herself. Finding Findabhair was not the sole reason for her search. Deep inside was a secret grief that she too had not been spirited away.

Mattie was watching her closely and nodded with sympathy. "You must take care, my dear. Before you go to find your cousin be certain of your motives. Otherwise both of you could be lost forever."

Gwen mulled over his words as she helped herself to a plate of shepherd's pie with marrow-fat peas. She was just finishing her dessert of sherry trifle when Mattie's secretary came for her. An older woman with short curly hair and glasses, she was casually dressed in slacks and a summer blouse.

"Don't rush yourself if you're not ready," she said.

"Oh I am, thanks. I hope this isn't an inconvenience."

"Not at all. I like to get away from my desk."

In the car, Gwen asked the secretary about Mattie's position in the company.

"He's the boss. The managing director. Didn't you know?"

Gwen was surprised. "He must be very nice to work for."

"An absolute dote. The best there is. Not like the shower who ran the place before him. We were a branch of a big foreign concern, but they pulled out of the country as soon as it looked like they were going to be taxed. That happens often enough here, let me tell you. We were closing down with all jobs lost when Mattie got the workers together to buy shares and form a cooperative. He was the sales rep before and now he's the top man, more power to him."

Gwen was let out at a junction and shown the road to take. Standing on the verge with her thumb out, she felt the optimism rise within her like bubbles of laughter. All by herself she had travelled this far, made a new friend and eaten a good meal. And now she was well on her way to meet up with Findabhair. Everything was going to work out fine. In a country where bosses chased sheep off their lawns and talked about fairies as if they lived next door, how could it not?

Chapter eight

The Burren is a rocky table-land embedded in the green countryside like a stone. A glacial sculpture thousands of years old, it has the appearance of a lunar landscape. The ground is encrusted with limestone pavements. The mountains are ribbed with stone terraces. Huge boulders lie in stony fields. Even the farmers' fences are made of stone, grey lace woven around every meadow. With the coming of summer the rock garden blooms. Miniature flowers peep out from crack and crevice: orchids of snow-white, speckled purple and pink; blue gentian and mountain aven; the burnet rose and dark-red helleborine. The air is bright with butterflies like tiny flowers themselves.

Into this strange bubble of speckled stone, Gwen arrived on foot. As Mattie had predicted, she had no trouble travelling through County Clare, but once inside the Burren she was on her own. The solitude was unsettling. After an hour's hike with only wildlife for company, she was beginning to wonder if she were the only person alive. She knew she was on the right track as occasional signposts pointed to Carron, but even without them she would have been confident. If ever there was a place suitable for fairies, this landscape was it.

At last she came to a crossroads where there was a little public house called Críode na Boirne. Inside, it was cool and dim with only two people, an old man at the counter sipping black stout and the young boy who was serving. Gwen bought a cola and a packet of peanuts as they sold no other food.

"Is this Carron?" she asked the boy.

"It is. Are you on your way to the Quirkes'?"

"No," she said, unsure where she was going now that she had arrived. "Is there some kind of meeting place around here that has a banquet hall?"

The old man coughed into his pint while the boy fought to keep a straight face.

"You're a long way from a fancy hotel," he said. "If you need a place to stop, you could try the Field Station. Through the village and first turn on your right. Students from the college stay there."

Laughter followed behind Gwen as she left the pub.

"A banquet hall no less," the old man was saying. "They're a ham sandwich short of a picnic, them Yanks."

Gwen refused to be discouraged. She was in the right place and she had a few hours yet to find what she was looking for. Twilight was the appointed time and the sky was still bright and sunny. With renewed determination, she set off once more.

Maybe someone at the Field Station can help me, she thought.

Her hopes were soon dashed when she reached the small white building standing alone outside the village of Carron. It was closed and deserted. Gwen gazed up the road ahead of her. As far as the eye could see, there was nothing but fields of stone and hazel scrub. A high ridge swept upwards to her right like a green ocean wave. In the distance, the sun glinted on the stony summits of the mountains so that they appeared to be covered in snow. A strong wind blew over the terrain with a soft hollow roar as if the rocks were hawing. Exhausted, downhearted, she felt like roaring back. What was she going to do now?

And as if the situation weren't bad enough, she was starving.

Gwen was about to return to the village to buy some provisions when something strange happened. From overhead came the whirr of a sparrowhawk's dive, and it seemed that someone called her name.

"What?" said Gwen, shielding her eyes as she looked up.

The hawk dove again, this time almost touching her with its wing. She ducked in panic.

"Okay, okay, you've got my attention!" she shouted, thankful that no one else was about.

While one part of her was seriously questioning her sanity, another was simply following Mattie's advice. *Pay attention to any voices you might hear out of the blue.*

Abruptly the bird left her. It flew over a nearby field and screeched raucously before diving down. Something caught? But no. Something called. There was a flash of bright orange as a fox streaked out from the hazel brush. He stepped onto the road just ahead of Gwen and stood and stared at her. Gwen moved toward him cautiously. The fox swished his tail. A little closer now, but he leaped away, back into the field yet staying in sight.

Am I loop-de-loo or what? Gwen asked herself as she scrambled through a hedge to follow him.

Though the fox went at a reasonable pace, it was rough going through those stony fields. Gwen had to watch her footing on the broken limestone pavements and avoid the sudden grykes that fissured the ground. It was all the more awkward with her knapsack, which was beginning to feel as if it were packed with Burren rocks. Though at first she had been interested in where she was going, eventually she marched blindly just to keep up. Her throat was parched, she felt light-headed, and the glare of sun on stone was hurting her eyes. But at last the trek ended as they came to a new road. The fox jumped onto the stone wall that bordered the field. Gwen hauled herself over it and onto the tarmac. The ground swayed beneath her feet. The landscape seemed askew. She knew she was suffering from fatigue and hunger, but there were no houses in sight where she could ask for help.

"Well done, Only-Two-Legs," barked the fox.

Gwen felt dizzy. Was he really talking to her? She leaned against the wall.

"We sensed you needed a friend," he said. "There is one nearby."

"Thank . . . thank you," Gwen managed to stammer before he disappeared over the wall with a final swish of his tail.

And what kind of friend does he mean? Gwen closed her eyes briefly. She was so worn out it took her a moment to react when shouts rang out.

In the field opposite her, a good way up from the road, a farmer was waving to her from a stone enclosure. Cows were ambling out of the enclosure and making their way toward her.

"Stand fast so they'll go ahead of you!" the farmer shouted again.

There was an open gate in the wall just beyond Gwen, and she realized with horror that the cattle were heading for it. A true city girl, she was unfamiliar with farm animals and terrified by their size. Frozen to the spot, not knowing what to do, she was sure they would suddenly stampede and kill her.

The first to come through, a black-and-white bullock, simply turned away from Gwen and loped up the road. The next did the same and on followed the rest till Gwen saw that she was sending them in the right direction by just standing there.

Accompanied by a sheepdog, the farmer came last. A young woman in her early twenties, she wore blue jeans streaked with mud, high wellington boots and a faded shirt. An old cap rested on a mass of red hair. In her hand she held a hazel switch, which she thwacked lightly over the rear ends of her cattle.

"Thanks for the hand," she said brightly to Gwen. "This lazy thing should have been doing the job, but he's too tired to run ahead sometimes. Ready for your pension, aren't you, Bran?" She scratched the ears of the dog, who whined apologetically. Then she put out her hand to grip Gwen's. "Kathleen Quirke. Call me Katie or call me quirky. Are you on your way to my house?"

Gwen introduced herself. "I don't know. They asked me that in the pub too. Do you run a hostel?"

Katie laughed. She was a handsome strong-featured girl with green eyes that sparkled with humour and intelligence. Much taller than Gwen, tanned and sinewy from outdoor work, she exuded health and high spirits.

"You could call it that. We take in Woofers, Will-ing Workers on Organic Farms. They're always arriv-ing on the doorstep—Americans, Germans, Italians, English. They work on the farm for a while and we feed and house them."

"Only foreigners? No Irish?"

Katie smirked. "You wouldn't catch the Irish working for nothing; they've more sense. Have you got a light? I'm down to my last match and saving it."

"Sorry, I don't smoke."

"Neither do I. Much."

Katie took a half-used butt from her shirt pocket and cupped her hands to protect the flame. Some of the cows had wandered up the road, but most stood nibbling the grass on the verge, waiting patiently for their mistress. She looked set for a long and leisurely conversation, but Gwen put an end to that by swaying suddenly in a near faint.

"What's the matter?" Katie demanded, all concern. She caught hold of Gwen, whose face had gone white.

"I . . . I'm okay," Gwen said, steadying herself. "It's my own fault. I haven't eaten for a while and I've been walking for miles."

"The house isn't far from here. We'll soon fix you up."

Ignoring her protests, Katie took Gwen's knapsack and slung it over her own shoulders as if it were empty. Then she linked her arm in Gwen's. "Lean on me if you get dizzy again."

"Sorry to be such a nuisance," Gwen said miserably.

"Don't be silly. I'd be a poor Christian if it were a bother to help someone."

Together they made their way slowly up the road,

Katie herding the cattle before her with low cries and the occasional flick of her stick.

"We're nearly there now. I'll just hunt these lads into the Maher Buídhe and we'll be home in a trice."

At last they reached the Quirke home, a big farmhouse with a thatched roof, on the side of a mountain. A few white goats wandered in the front yard where an old tractor stood idle. Rows of green vegetables grew in a walled garden to the side. Behind the house were sheds and a cattle yard, overshadowed by a hay barn.

"The car's gone," Katie commented, looking around. "Mam and the girls must be counting sheep."

The first room in the house was a wide shady living space. A mahogany dining table dominated the floor. The television was perched on top of a piano. Rugs and mats were scattered in front of the fat sofa and armchairs. By the fireplace, on a hearth of flagstones, was a woven pannier filled with sods of turf. On the walls were photographs of the family, going back generations.

Gwen felt immediately comforted by the sense of "home." It was like a mother's embrace after all her hardship.

"Sit you down while I get us a bite to eat," Katie ordered, bustling into the kitchen.

In no time she returned with a feast of cold ham and chicken, potato salad and a plate heaped with buttered bread. The two of them tucked in without a word, washing down the meal with mugs of hot tea. When she was full, Gwen sat back with a sigh, totally revived.

"That's better." Katie grinned with satisfaction. "You were white as a ghost. I thought you were going to faint on me and I'd have to put you up on the black limousine. He's pure wild. Might have run off with you into the mountains."

She let out a laugh but Gwen looked puzzled.

"Limousine? I didn't see a car."

Katie spluttered and laughed louder. "A limousine is a breed of cattle. You're a right eejit."

Gwen laughed too. She didn't mind Katie's making fun of her. The older girl was already something of a heroine to her. "I don't know how to thank you," she began.

Katie waved away her words. "Listen, you're to stop here tonight and get a good rest. You can help me with a few things tomorrow before going on your way, or you can stay as long as you like. We'll make a Woofer out of you. What do you think?"

It sounded wonderful to Gwen. To become friends with Katie and meet her family. To work outdoors on the farm, maybe in the garden, or even with the animals. Just to stay in one place for a while, instead of roaming alone around the countryside.

"I'd love to, believe me," she said sadly, "but I can't. It's difficult to explain. I was travelling with my cousin and she . . . we went different ways. I'm supposed to meet her somewhere around here, but the, uh, arrangements we made are sort of vague."

Katie nodded sympathetically. "You had a row? That's bound to happen when two people travel together. Don't worry, you'll be friends again when you meet up. A little time away makes all the difference."

"Yes," said Gwen with guilty relief, leaving matters as they stood. Though she liked Katie, Gwen was reluctant to tell the whole story. Mattie had been easier because he was so much older, but Katie was closer in age. Gwen didn't want to look foolish.

"But the problem is—where will I find her? There's supposed to be a banquet hall or a place where a banquet might be held, somewhere near Carron. Not a modern place, I think. Something old or even ancient. That's what we've been touring around to see."

"There's a ruined castle at Leamanagh," Katie suggested. "Maire Ruadh's great house. She was the wife of an O'Brien chieftain who was killed in the Cromwellian wars and she married an English officer so her sons could keep their land. The castle isn't far from here, but I haven't heard tell of any stories about banquets or feasts there. Something ancient," she muttered to herself. Then her face lit up. "The Fulacht Fia! Could that be it? The Ancient Eating Place on the Boston Road. You would have passed near it, just outside the village."

"Ancient Eating Place," Gwen said excitedly. "That must be it! I'm sorry to be rude, but I'll clean up and then I must go. I'm supposed to be there by twilight!"

Katie caught her urgency and glanced out the window. The sun was setting over the Burren, inflaming the stony mountains with a red and orange glow.

"Never mind the delft—we'll wash up later. I'll take you on my motorbike. Let's go!"

Chapter Nine

═══════════════════════════════════════

The motorbike bucked and leaped like a colt as Katie sped down the narrow road, oblivious to the potholes. Behind her, Gwen clung on for dear life as they dipped into curves and swerved past stone walls. The sun was already low in the sky. Was she too late? When exactly was twilight?

Katie drew up the bike at a lonely signpost that appeared to be pointing at nothing but an empty field.

Fulacht Fia. Ancient Eating Place.

"There isn't much to see," she said to Gwen as she took off her helmet. "Just a grassy circle and a few stones. It would have been where a Celtic tribe ate their communal meals."

"Or some other 'tribe,' " Gwen murmured.

"Are you sure she'll come? What if this isn't the right place? I'll wait with you."

"No!" Gwen said, with more emphasis than she intended. She spoke quickly to fend off Katie's dismay. "It is the right place. And it's not that I don't appreciate your offer, but this is something I have to do alone."

The older girl was not convinced. She pointed to the dark clouds that were gathering over the mountains.

"There could be a storm tonight. They're pure wild in the summertime. If you think I'm going to leave you out alone—"

"You don't know what's going on," Gwen said in a panic, sensing that Katie was digging in her heels. "I hardly know myself. It could be dangerous. I can't drag you into it."

Even as she argued, Gwen could see she was taking the wrong tack. Excitement flickered in Katie's green eyes. She was the impulsive kind, a woman of action. Very like Findabhair, in fact. That made up Gwen's mind. She didn't need another one lost in Fairyland.

"No," Gwen said again, in a voice that was both quiet and final. "The farm needs you. Your family needs you. I won't say anything more except that this is my battle. Please let me handle it myself."

Gwen had got it right this time. Though she did so reluctantly, Katie gave in at last.

"Fair enough. We all have our own patch to plough. I won't interfere with yours. Good luck to you, whatever it is you're facing. I gather you haven't told me everything, but that's your business. Remember now, if you need me, you know where I am."

As the motorbike disappeared down the road, Gwen felt the loneliness settle over her like a cloak. She would have liked to have Katie with her, but she felt she had made the right decision.

Gwen stepped over the stile that led into the field and followed a worn path in the knee-high grass. It brought her to a green hollow rimmed with white stones half-buried in the earth. Alone in the great silence of the Burren night, she sat down and waited.

When it happened, it happened immediately, as if the other world had shaken itself awake with a roar.

Their arrival was like a blast of wind, a great soft blow. They poured into the hollow like molten silver. Almost indescribable in human terms. Almost invisible to mortal eyes. Their silhouettes against the dark sky hinted of slender graceful shapes, but they were so amorphous as to appear also like falling water or columns of pure light. They were translucent, and transparent too, for Gwen could see the contours of the landscape through them. Did they have wings? Or was that the moonlight trailing behind them? They moved with such breathtaking swiftness that wings, tresses, pale limbs were all the same it seemed. They danced in the circle, singing with wild glee.

Paralyzed, Gwen sat wide-eyed and watching. She was seized by a wonder that was also terror. These were not human. Not of the world she knew. Their very presence was shattering. Unable to stop herself, she uttered a cry.

The madcap chatter ceased abruptly. Trembling like moonbeams, the glorious creatures stood still.

"There is a mortal amongst us!" a voice cried out. It sounded like the wail of the wind.

"What brought this human here?" another hissed, as if water doused flame.

Gwen wanted to answer, to explain and apologize, but she felt so heavy beside their lightness, like a great lump of stone or a sod of earth. Sphinx-like she sat, solemn and dumbstruck, staring at the eyes that stared back like stars.

They gathered around her and peered into her face. She was being crowded by mist and will-o'-the-wisps. Some touched her curiously with little strokes. One blew into her mouth and ears. She shivered at their touch but was unable to move or speak.

"She has never seen us before. She is fairy-struck."

Their whispers were like the rustle of leaves, the creaking of branches. They were calmer now as they saw she was helpless.

"A golden-haired girl," one of them said softly, "with a face as pale as the moon. She is a pretty mortal. Shall we take her with us?"

"Here is our captain! He will know."

Though Gwen could barely discern one shape from another—they all flashed and flickered like fireworks—she was able to see the beautiful youth who approached her. His hair fell like moonlight over his shoulders, and a golden circlet shone on his brow.

"Wouldst thou come to our banquet, fair Gwen-hyvar?"

She didn't stop to wonder how he knew her name. The word "banquet" was like a charm that set her free. With a gasp she remembered why she had come and she leaped to her feet.

"Is it here? Where's Findabhair?"

The shining youth shook his head. "She is not here, dear one. You were led astray by that mischievous leprechaun who is in league with the King. In fair sport he should have directed you to our mountain. But you came close enough that we could aid you. I have brought my own troop to bring you thither."

With that, he suddenly shot upwards like a comet returning to the sky. And his voice rang out to command the night. "Get me a horse!"

The others immediately took up his cry.

"Come fairy steeds from the Caves of the Wild Horses!"

Their shouts resounded over the Burren to the caves where the fairy steeds dwelt. Out came the wild horses from their craggy stable, like a rush of wind rolling down the mountains.

Gwen saw them in the clouds, racing past the moon. Arched necks and broad chests and huge eyes like opals. Stars glittered in their manes which swept behind them like wings. Hooves thundered across the sky as they galloped toward the fairy folk. Rearing up on hind legs and tossing their heads, they snorted defiantly and dared anyone to ride them.

The fairies were quick to take up the challenge. They ran with the horses and caught on to their manes. Some succeeded in mounting with one fleet jump. Others were flung away to somersault in the air like pinwheels. Still others, unable to take their seat, raced alongside, arms entangled in horsehair, screeching with laughter and mock pleas for mercy.

Gwen quaked inside. This wild abandon, this utter madness, was beyond anything imaginable. It was a nightmare she had no hope of controlling. Exquisite chaos. Again she was overwhelmed by the terrifying truth. All these beings, both riders and steeds, were supernatural. They shouldn't exist.

And yet, there was something inside her, some vague, restless and exiled part of her, which recognized them. Remembered them. In the deep ocean of her subconscious, the dreamer stirred. She wavered between the huge fear of what might happen if she joined them and the equally huge fear of being left behind.

No kind hand was proffered to help her mount. She knew in her heart she would have to do it alone.

Courage is not lack of fear; it is acting despite the fear.

The words whispered deep within her. Her soul fluttered like a small bird in a cage, yearning to be free.

With a leap of faith, Gwen ran toward a high-stepping mare whose golden-brown colouring was the same as her own.

"You are for me!" she cried.

The horse reared up in response, but as soon as the hooves touched the earth again Gwen took her chance. She jumped forward to grasp the long mane and flung one leg over the shining bare back. The mare bucked ferociously to toss her away. Half-up, half-down, Gwen flapped in midair like a paper bag in the wind. But she refused to let go and gritted her teeth, determined to hold on even if she were trampled to death.

Sensing the iron will of her hapless rider, the fairy steed went suddenly quiet. In that moment of sweet stillness, Gwen righted herself.

She patted the mare's neck with relief and respect. "Thank you, lady," she whispered into an elegant ear.

The mare whinnied in reply.

A jubilant shout rose from the fairy troop, all seated now.

"Ride fast! Ride fast! The spell is cast!"

CHAPTER TEN

Oh, the exhilaration of that night ride over the Burren! It was like riding the wind. Silver-shod hooves rode the currents of air as if they were the smooth sward of a race-course. Triumphantly one of the glorious host, Gwen felt like a goddess. Eyes shining with fairy sight, she gazed on the landscape below her with intimate know-ledge.

Over Cahercommaun they flew, a massive stone fort on the edge of a cliff. It was no longer the empty ruin that stood in her own time. Gwen could see smoke rising from within the ramparts. Among wood and stone houses strode a tall people clothed in bright linen. Jewelled brooches clasped their mantles, and golden torques shone round their necks. Warriors practised with the clash of iron. Both men and women were of a high proud countenance.

"All hail!" cried the fairies as they passed by. "All hail to the ancient tribes of Erin!"

They sped on to Leamanagh Castle, where lights shone from mullioned windows as Maire Ruadh dined her guests. Unbowed by defeat, she wooed her English conqueror with a toss of her long red hair. In the passage of time her plans would succeed. Her sons would be chieftains like their murdered father.

"Our blessings upon you, lion-hearted Mary!"

On dashed the cavalcade, beneath the sky of stars. Over cairn and cashel, over bog and rushy pasture, over runnelled rock meadow and holy well. From that marvellous height, Gwen saw a new aspect of the Burren mountains. Where lush grasses were hidden on the stony terraces, they came into view from the air like a sea of rolling green. And with her magical sight she could see also the secrets that lay under the earth: subterranean rivers, a honeycomb of caves and the labyrinth of turloughs that flowed underground, waiting to rise up like lakes at the first heavy rain.

When they reached the majestic Poulnabrone Dolmen, standing alone in a field of stone, the fairies swooped down. Inside the sheltering walls of the cromlech, two lovers lay fast asleep. Their beautiful young faces showed hunger and hardship; yet there was no sign of regret for the love that had made them fugitives from the Fianna and Finn MacCool.

A hush fell over the fairy folk, solemn-eyed like worshippers at a wayside shrine. They laid gifts of food at the lovers' feet and covered their cold limbs with sheepskin rugs. The night wind echoed with their whispering.

"Sweet Diarmuid and Gráinne. We who were ancient in ancient days grant thee a night's peace from the din of men and the hunters' hounds."

The young couple stirred in each other's arms and smiled in their sleep.

Airborne once more, Gwen could have ridden forever. She had left behind all memory of her ordinary self. There was only the night wind and the flight of the wild horses and the company of a shining angelic folk. Then they flew over a human dwelling. With a start, Gwen recognized the thatched roof of the Quirke home. Bran was asleep on the doorstep, but he suddenly lifted his head to bay. Inside the house, the family turned in their sleep as if they too sensed the hosting pass by.

For Gwen, it was an uncomfortable reminder of something forgotten.

"I'm human," she whispered with sad surprise.

A warning sounded faintly in the back of her mind. A man's voice echoed from far away. *You must take care, my dear. Otherwise both of you could be lost forever.*

As they crossed over a steep gorge, the fairy troop began to descend. For a moment Gwen thought they were going to crash into the side of a cliff, but then she saw the wide crack in the mountain. With a rush of wings and wind, they landed inside.

When the company dismounted, Gwen noticed the change in the fairies. They were no longer shadowy beings of light, but were solid and human-like while strikingly beautiful. The fairy captain who had invited her to the banquet approached. He appeared now to be a handsome young man with dark-red hair.

"My name is Midir. Do not fear and no harm will befall you. Only take no food or wine that may be offered to you, if you wish to reach your world again."

He beckoned her to follow and after a moment's hesitation Gwen did. Though she no longer fully believed in the leprechaun's words, he had been right so far about red-haired people.

Midir led her deep into the cave. A damp clay musk, the perfume of stone, hung in the air and made her throat catch. There was the constant sound of dripping water. The walls and roof of solid rock were ribbed and rippled like a muscled body. Before long they came to a flight of steps that went further underground. Gwen was beginning to wonder if she would ever see daylight again, when they passed through an archway into a fabulous hall.

The hollow of the mountain, it was of immense size, with a floor of purple amethyst, and columns of fluorspar entwined with green garlands. A thousand candles lit up the gallery from chandeliers that were like fountains of crystal. Silken tapestries covered the walls. Their embroidered scenes depicted a beautiful country: honey-gold mountains and milk-white streams, and bright birds in the branches of apple-blossom trees. Gwen wondered if it were the Garden of Eden. Did the fairies still have what her own race had lost? But she didn't have time to muse. Her senses were being bombarded by every kind of marvel.

The fairy folk assembled in the hall were as splendid as their court. Of every shape and size and colour, each more exquisite than the next, they were resplendent in an utter extravagance of fashion: flounces of silk and satin; swaths of frosted lace; billowing mantles and floor-length trains; high-plumed hats and jewelled fans; clothes sewn with seed pearls and stippled with gems; tiaras shedding veils; necklaces and bracelets glittering with diamonds. Gwen blinked. She had stepped into a fairy tale! She would have stood there gaping all night if Findabhair hadn't come running to embrace her with joy.

"You got here! Well done, cuz. I thought that rascal might play tricks on you. The King, I mean. He couldn't make up his mind whether he wanted you here or not. I had no way of reaching you. We've been on the move since Tara. God, it's been madness. Parties day and night. These people are daft. I feel like I've died and gone to heaven!"

"So you're okay."

CHAPTER ELEVEN

Gwen had only to look at Findabhair to see that she was no suffering captive. In contrast to the riotous fairy colours, she wore a gown of midnight black shot through with silver. Her long hair, more golden now, was plaited in four locks with a diamond drop at the end of each tress. Eyes bright with laughter, cheeks flushed like two roses, she was obviously having the time of her life.

But her high spirits faded at Gwen's cool reception and she was immediately anxious. "Has it been hard for you? Oh Gwen, I'm so sorry. I agreed to go without really thinking. I had no idea you wouldn't come too."

Confused by her cousin's words, Gwen was already relenting her own bad humour. Though she had been worried about Findabhair, she had to admit she hadn't really suffered either. The adventure around Ireland

and the friends she had met were well worth the trouble. So why this anger?

"What do you mean I wouldn't come too?" she demanded.

Aware that something was wrong between them, Findabhair spoke frankly. "Finvarra said so. The King of the Fairies. His name is like mine, isn't that brilliant? Apparently my spirit agreed to go wholeheartedly— what can I say, that's me—but some part of you resisted and by fairy law he couldn't take you. He was annoyed at that, let me tell you, as he wanted the two of us, the cheeky thing. Fairies are not monogamous by any stretch of the imagination."

Findabhair burst out laughing. Gwen had to grin. Her cousin was "pure wild," as Katie would say. But it was what she said that eased Gwen's mind, for it removed the hurt she had been nursing secretly. So she hadn't been left behind after all! She hadn't been rejected by the fairy folk. Her own nature had refused to go. Gwen's grin widened when she realized why.

"I guess Canadians are too practical to go 'wholeheartedly' into Gagaland."

The two girls laughed together. All was well between them again.

"You're still in black. You look terrific." Gwen frowned at her own muddied blue jeans and jacket, feeling very out of place in those glittering surroundings.

"Finvarra loves black too," said Findabhair, "being

Lord of the Night and what-have-you. Say a colour and I'll work a bit of magic on you. Not pink or I'll gag."

"Oh, come on," Gwen said sceptically, but it was worth a try. "Well, if I can't have pink, how about a passionate red and some of that silver stuff you've got?"

"Excellent! You're getting more daring, old girl."

With a big smile and a wave of her hand, Findabhair sprinkled her cousin with starry dust. Gwen gasped at the transformation. Clouds of orange-red satin floated to the ground, trimmed with a silver fringe. Rubies winked on her ears and throat.

"Wow!" Gwen said in ecstasy. "How did you do that?"

"Fairy glamour," Findabhair replied nonchalantly. "None of this is real, you know. We could be standing here starkers, if the truth were known."

"Thanks. I need that thought like a hole in the head."

In fact, Gwen wasn't going to worry about the finer details. She felt like Cinderella who had finally reached the ball and she was going to make the most of it before the clock struck twelve. But it was Findabhair's turn to be serious. She took Gwen's arm and drew her away to a secluded corner of the hall.

"Listen, I've got to talk to you before Finvarra gets here. I have to be careful in case he hears."

"Married already, are you?"

"Ha ha. But this is no joke, Gwen. He's a tricky divil. Don't underestimate him. And he thinks he's God's gift to women. I'm cooling his heels a bit, though it's not easy I don't mind telling you. And he really fancies me. But at the same time, he's not happy that you escaped him. I know he wants to get back at you, but I don't know how. You've got to watch your step."

"Is this a big game or what?"

"Life is a game for the fairies, Gwen. Feasting and frolic, music and dancing. They've been here since the world began, but they never grow old and I'd say they never grow up."

"Permanent teenagers," Gwen said with awe.

"That's the story," Findabhair agreed, laughter bubbling up again. "And that's why I love them. But you have to keep in mind, they are not like us. They don't have the same kind of feelings. Guilt is something they've never known, which might be fine for some, but it means they can get away with murder without batting an eyelid."

"You seem to know them pretty well."

"To live with them is to know them," Findabhair declared, then she added lightly, "and I am their Queen, for what it's worth."

Gwen couldn't help but laugh. "You might think I've changed, but you have too. You sound a lot more sensible."

"When everyone else around you is cracked, you have to keep a head on your shoulders."

A fanfare of trumpets suddenly blared through the hall. The music and dancing came to a halt.

"My lord and master is about to arrive," Findabhair said.

Despite the dry tone, Gwen could see that her cousin was barely keeping rein on a breathless excitement.

"Be careful yourself," she murmured with concern.

The lords and ladies of the fairy court bowed graciously as the King made his entrance. Dressed simply in black, a silken mantle tossed over his shoulders, he was a startling figure. His jet-black hair fell in a blunt cut reminiscent of ancient Egypt. And like a pharaoh's carved in stone, his features were finely chiselled, proud and exquisite. The almond-shaped eyes glowed as deep as dark velvet. Though his garments glimmered like the night, he wore no adornment other than the star that shone on his forehead.

"Isn't he gorgeous?" whispered Findabhair.

"Not my type, but I can see your point," said Gwen.

Finvarra's glance swept the court till it settled on the two girls. For a brief moment he regarded Gwen coolly, then his face lit up as he smiled at Findabhair. With an elegant gesture he extended his hand toward her, as melodious music filled the hall once more.

"I'm off to dance," Findabhair said hurriedly. "Behave yourself. I'll try to."

"Wait a minute! We haven't figured out—"

But Findabhair was already tripping lightly toward the King, catching up her skirts as they flounced around her. Wryly Gwen watched as the two spun in each other's arms like figurines on a music box.

"Wilt thou dance with me, lady?"

Midir bowed to Gwen with a quizzical look. But though her feet twitched as if to dance, Gwen was overcome by her usual shyness.

"I'm not very good," she said. "In fact, I'm hopeless. That's why I never go to clubs."

"It is not possible to stumble to fairy music," he assured her.

With serious misgivings, Gwen finally agreed, certain that she was about to make an idiot of herself. But Midir's words were true. With his arm around her waist, guiding her effortlessly, she found herself gliding over the floor like a swan. Surprised at how easy it was, she grew more confident. Letting the music sweep through her, a wild dash of a waltz, she was now twirling and swirling in the midst of the crowd. It was as if her feet had been loosed from chains. She was dancing on air. She was flying!

"This is fantastic! I really feel like Cinderella."

"I remember her. A charming girl."

"How could you? That's just a—"

"Fairy tale?"

They laughed together as they spun around the hall. It wasn't only the dancing that was new to Gwen, but talking so freely to a handsome young man as well. Was everything easier in Fairyland? And why couldn't she be like this in her own world?

"Will this lady grant me a dance?" came a voice behind her.

Though she would have preferred to stay with Midir, Gwen didn't want to be rude. "Okay," she said blithely, turning to face her new partner.

When she saw who it was, she nearly jumped with fright. But ready or not, he had caught hold of her.

Gwen was now dancing with the King of the Fairies.

CHAPTER TWELVE

Though she man-
aged to keep in step, Gwen was quaking inside. He had
caught her off guard. What would she say? Annoyed
that he could make her so nervous, she steadied herself, determined not to let him get the better of her.

"You have honoured my court with your presence, after all."

He spoke graciously.

Too gracious, she thought.

"No thanks to you or your leprechaun. I could still
be sitting in a dark wet field."

A spark flared in the King's eyes, but Gwen could-
n't tell if it was anger or amusement.

"You are of the same mettle as Findabhair. I did
not think so when first I saw you at Tara. She was the
briared rose, and you, the buttercup."

"The story of my life."

Her tone made him laugh, a rather delightful laugh, and he touched her chin.

"I love butter," he said.

It was the last thing she expected, this irresistible charm. She knew he was teasing her and she had to laugh. Her defences wobbled. Though she fought against it, she was beginning to like him.

Sensing her change of attitude, Finvarra smiled mischievously. "Perhaps you regret your refusal of me?"

"Maybe a tiny iota," she teased back, amazed at herself. This was flirting, wasn't it? Findabhair would kill her. "But it wouldn't work. I'm not into harems. And you're more Findabhair's type."

"Ah yes," the King sighed. He looked genuinely troubled. "We are well matched, your cousin and I. She leads me on a merry dance and I am fair bewitched by her."

He looked around the hall and spied his tormentor dancing in the arms of a blond giant.

"I shall return you to my *Tánaiste*, who seems quite enchanted himself. May I hope that we are on better terms?"

Gwen stared into the cat-like eyes that reflected the wisdom and wildness of millennia spent young. Despite herself, she found it impossible to deny him. A light kiss brushed her cheek and he bowed before leaving her.

Midir was quick to retrieve his partner. At his questioning look, Gwen could only shake her head.

"What can I say? I have met the enemy and he's Prince Charming."

"He is the King."

"And you're the *Tánaiste*? What does that mean?"

"I am his second-in-command. Though I am captain of my own troop and there are many like me, Finvarra is High King over all. If anything were to happen to him, I would rule in his place. But that is unlikely as we are, each of us, immortal."

Gwen caught her breath as his simple statement struck home. She was dancing with someone who would live forever! Like contemplating the size of the universe, it was almost too difficult to grasp. She wanted to know more about fairy life, but was distracted by a burst of fireworks over the hall. Tiny coloured birds and butterflies, fiery dragons and catherine wheels showered the air.

"It must be wonderful," she said, "to live with magic every day."

Midir regarded her carefully. "Would you like to stay with us, Gwenhyvar?"

Something in his voice told Gwen it was time to make her position clear, not only to him but to herself as well.

"I can't. It's out of the question. Even though a part of me wants to. It's all so weird. My entire life I've been looking for other worlds, and now here I've found one and it's so fantastic I can hardly believe it. But . . . but now I know that, at the most, I only ever meant to visit. I mean, even though I can't say I'm very happy in it, I never intended to reject my own world."

Midir nodded at her words, accepting them as final. "I would not hold you here against your will, but I cannot say the same of Finvarra. Take care. For your own sake and your cousin's."

A shiver ran up Gwen's back. She looked at the bright hall with a different eye. Was it a gilded cage? A beautiful prison? Had she been lulled into a false sense of security? What lay under the glamour and charm? She decided then and there it was time to stop the party. She would find Findabhair and tell her they must go home.

At that very moment, on the other side of the court, the King clapped his hands like the peal of a bell. "Let the feasting commence!"

In the twinkling of an eye a great banquet table appeared, covered with snow-white linen. Stretching the length of the hall, it was laid out with dishes of gold and silver and goblets of crystal rimmed with gems. Though she had already been dazzled by every kind of wonder, Gwen could hardly believe what her eyes now beheld.

Everything delicious and imaginable was spread out before her. The centre piece was a whole roasted pig with a juicy red apple clenched in its jaw. Beside it stood a shellfish fantasia like a castle of coral dripping with sea flowers. There were chickens stuffed with raisins and chestnuts, nests of quails' eggs and prawns, roast duck with shallots and mountains of pink lobster. Wheels of cheese were hemmed in by ham pies and beef pies and mince pies. Pyramids of fruit spilled into tiers of nuts, so that the soft ripe skins of grapes and cherries burst against the hard brown shells of filberts and walnuts. And oh, the side dishes! Pears dipped in melted cheddar. Crispy cucumber cups stuffed with crab meat. And every kind of mushroom. For the fairy folk love mushrooms and none are poisonous to them. White buttons and fat browns, red-speckled and yellow-frilled, some lay freshly picked in baskets while others swam in butter encrusted with garlic. As for the desserts, Gwen's knees went weak at the sight of them. Strawberries smothered in cream and dusted with brown sugar. Raspberries coated in chocolate and frosted with white sugar. Brittle towers of honeycomb filled with gobs of ice cream and topped with swirls of meringue. Stunning confections of marbled cake with layer upon layer upon layer of icing. There were gooseberry fools, cranberry and rhubarb jellies, melon jellies, green jellies of wild mint.

And a cold dark chocolate mousse that frothed like cream.

Inside Gwen, alarm bells were ringing. She knew she was facing her most perilous test. Had the King sensed that food was her soft spot? The feast laid out was temptation itself.

At the head of the table, Findabhair tried to catch her cousin's attention but was unable to move or cry out in warning. Beside her, Finvarra sat with stately poise, dark eyes narrowed and a sleek smile on his lips. A cat watching a mouse.

"Eat no food and drink no wine if you wish to return to your home again."

Midir's whisper was urgent as he passed behind her.

Gwen groaned with the unfairness of the trial. All her favourite foods were there, sparkling with just that extra touch of deliciousness that attends the forbidden. (Isn't this what happened to poor Adam and Eve?) The hot dishes wafted rich scents toward her. The cold dishes glinted and winked with enticement.

Gwen shuddered and then sighed.

"I'll have a little bit of everything, please."

CHAPTER THIRTEEN

With her mind made up, Gwen rushed to the table. In a matter of seconds her plate was heaped high. A hush had fallen over the assembly. All eyes watched as she savoured her first bite.

Heaven. Ambrosia. Food of the gods.

She had no sooner swallowed than the company broke into uproarious applause. Findabhair sank back in her chair with dismay. Finvarra leaped to his feet. The black cloak swirled behind him as he raised his arms in triumph. The star in the centre of his forehead flashed.

"The lady hath failed her trial! She is ours!"

Though the proclamation was met with riotous approval, it appeared the judgement was not unanimous. Ever mercurial and capricious in their humours, the fairy folk began to argue amongst themselves. As the feast got under way, voices of dissent were heard amidst the talk and laughter.

"She was the victor in the first test," Midir called out. "She tamed her night mare. Our claim is not pure."

Cheers and "Hear! Hear!" echoed from various quarters. Piqued by the challenge of one so high as the *Tánaiste*, those loyal to the King responded with catcalls. The bright lords and ladies were now seriously at odds.

Some cried, "Unfair," "Poor sport, this," while others, equally vehement, chanted, "She is ours, she is ours." Many were genuinely upset. Many more were convulsed with laughter. One portly red-cheeked fellow was holding his sides as if they might split with his guffaws. A twinkling sprite stood on her chair to make herself heard. A leprechaun had taken off his hornpipe shoe and was banging it on the table. Two pixies had resorted to fisticuffs. The more serene of the elphin folk shook their golden locks and tapped cutlery against crystal to make a disgruntled noise.

As the assembly grew more agitated, the disharmony spilled over into their environment. All the jellies began to quiver. Dishes hopped on the table. Ice cubes rattled in the punch bowls. Stoppers popped from the decanters of wine. The chandeliers began to sway and a thousand candles flickered and spat. As if thoroughly disgusted with the whole affair, the roast pig stood up on its haunches, got down from the banquet and marched out of the hall. The furniture itself began to twitch as if it too wanted to leave. The very structure of the hall turned this way and that, shaken by the indecision of its occupants.

Pandemonium reigned.

Only two people seemed unaffected by the chaos: Findabhair, who was still trying to catch Gwen's attention, looking both amused and chagrined; and Gwen herself, the centre of the controversy, eating away in a state of bliss.

Finvarra and Midir were now arguing vociferously, each backed by the shouts of their factions. It couldn't continue. Too much power was unleashed in the course of their frenzy. The hall began to pitch and toss like a ship on a wild sea. Everything was sent flying through the air—furniture, feast and even the fairies themselves.

The last thing Gwen remembered was the dish of chocolate mousse, which she caught sailing past her. She managed only one hearty scoop before she too was hurled upwards.

Then she awoke.

On the hillside of the Burren's Glen of Clab.

In the middle of the worst storm imaginable.

Stunned by her abrupt expulsion from the hall, Gwen was hardly ready for a violent storm. The night was black and raging. Rain poured from the sky. Wind and water lashed the hillside. Whips of lightning cracked overhead, followed by threatening claps of thunder. It was as if the elemental hounds of hell had been unleashed upon the land.

There was no time to think about what had happened. Her immediate need was shelter. Gwen made her way down the hillside. The stony slope of the gorge was slippery and treacherous. She was scraped and bruised by the time she reached the bottom. A miserable figure, wet and bedraggled, she came at last to the road beyond the glen.

There she was met by more mayhem. Cattle charged toward her, wild-eyed and panic-stricken. Behind them, at snail's pace, a car drove them onwards. Running alongside the car were Katie and two younger girls, all in shining yellow macks. With shouts and sharp sticks, the girls controlled the cows who were trying to break through the stone walls and into the fields.

Katie ran up to Gwen. "Ho girl! This is no night to be out!"

Beneath the hood of her mack, Katie's face was aglow with excitement. Obviously she looked on the storm as a challenge and was in full command.

"I don't suppose I could help?" Gwen offered half-heartedly.

"We're putting these lads with the others at the Maher Buídhe. They'll be more sheltered there, poor things. They want to hide under the trees, the most dangerous spot with the lightning. I don't think you'd be of any use, Gwen; they're pure wild with fright. Go to the house. The electricity is off but there's a fire in the grate. If you'd like to help, make us something hot for when we get back."

"I will," Gwen promised.

Before she departed, Katie stared into Gwen's face for a moment. She was about to say something, but thunder pealed overhead. The terrified bellows of the cattle followed soon after. There was no time to talk. Katie ran down the road after the strays that had bolted.

When Gwen reached the house, she found all in near darkness. The electricity had been knocked out by the storm. Candles flickered in saucers to provide a dim light. Where the thatched roof was raining in patches, buckets and pots caught the drips. In the kitchen, more basins plonked to the tune of falling water. Under the table, the dog cowered from the thunder like a frightened child.

"It's okay, Bran," Gwen said soothingly, but he stared back at her with the dumb terror of beasts.

She dried herself at the kitchen range, then rummaged around for ingredients to make a soup. Glad of something to keep herself occupied, she didn't want to think just yet about her disaster in Fairyland. But as the vegetables and herbs simmered in the pot, the pleasant smell of simple fare was a damning reminder. Only a short while ago she had eaten her fill of food far richer. Her stomach felt queasy, as if she had devoured a huge box of chocolates all in one go.

There's work to be done, she told herself quickly, thinking of the Quirke women out battling the elements.

She set out dishes on the table in the living room. The hearth fire had died down, so she built it up again with sods of turf. Having done all she could for the moment, she sank into a big chair and dozed fitfully.

The evening's events were taking their toll. Gwen felt drained and feverish. The candles in the room confused her, harking back to the fairy hall. Outside the window, the Burren mountains were blue-black and shining, like whales sailing through a storm-driven sea. The wind howled over the house with the wail of the banshee. Everything seemed formless and chaotic.

At last she heard the car coming up the driveway and Gwen roused herself to put on the kettle for tea.

When the Quirkes came in, shaking off their wet macks, their worn faces brightened at the scene before them. Bowls of piping-hot soup were laid on the table with plates of sandwiches and a big pot of tea.

Katie introduced her mother and sisters.

"The fire blazing and all," Mrs. Quirke said warmly. "You're a most welcome guest, my dear."

While the others enjoyed their supper, Gwen took only a light cup of tea.

"Not eating?" Katie enquired with a deliberate stare.

Gwen looked away. "I've had too much tonight already."

Katie frowned but said nothing as the others chatted around the table.

"I've seen many a wild storm in my day," Mrs. Quirke stated, "but this beats all. You brought the bad weather with you, Gwen."

Though she knew it was merely an expression, Gwen flinched. Not for the first time that night she wondered if the storm was fairy fury and if she wasn't the cause of it.

It was later, when the spare bed had been set up in Katie's room and Gwen was about to fall asleep, that Katie questioned her. The older girl turned on the side lamp. The look on her face was one of grave concern.

"I don't want to offend you, Gwen, and maybe it's none of my business, but I'm going to ask you anyway. Are you taking drugs? Were you meeting a drug pedlar tonight?"

A strange lassitude had come over Gwen. Her mind felt as if it were wrapped in cotton wool, all soft and white. If Katie had asked her name she would have had to think about it. But the question was far more serious, though utterly absurd. While one part of Gwen wanted to laugh, another part of her felt like crying. Katie was acting like a big sister. She obviously cared about Gwen.

"They don't deal in drugs," Gwen answered slowly. "They deal in dreams. Perhaps it has the same effect?"

Katie would have demanded an explanation but Gwen put an end to their talk by simply falling fast asleep.

CHAPTER FOURTEEN

━━━━━━━━━━━━━━━━━━━━━━━━━━━━━━

The next morning Gwen awoke to find Katie sitting in a chair by her bed.

"This must be what a hangover feels like," she groaned.

Her throat was parched, she felt hot and achy, and her head throbbed as if it housed an orchestra of hammers and tongs.

"You mean you don't know?" Katie asked, her look of concern changing to a grin.

"Nope. I've never taken drugs, to answer your last question, and that includes alcohol. Boy, do I feel awful." She sat up shakily.

"You had a rough night," Katie said quietly. "Fever and bad dreams. Mam said to call the doctor if you didn't improve today. I'm really ashamed of myself. You were acting so odd, but I didn't think you were coming down with something. I'm a right *amadán*."

"I don't know what that is but I'm sure you're not." Gwen managed a smile. "You were right to be suspicious, but it's not what you thought it was."

A silence fell between the girls, resonant with unspoken questions and answers. Katie didn't want to burden Gwen with her curiosity, though she knew some mystery was afoot. Gwen, in turn, was debating on how much she would tell Katie. After the fiasco at the fairy banquet, she badly needed advice. She had no idea what to do next.

"I'm going to ask you something, Katie," she said tentatively. It was a hunch, but she was thinking of Mattie and also of Katie's red hair. "It'll sound crazy, but I'm not joking. Okay?"

"You're on," said Katie. "I'm all ears."

"Do you believe in fairies?"

Katie's eyes widened, but she didn't laugh nor look scornful or bewildered.

"Yes," she said simply, to Gwen's huge relief. "Ever since I was a little girl. I still leave out a drop of the best milk on the windowsill at night, or some wine if we have it for dinner. It's an old tradition, a courtesy. The family thinks I'm daft but I do it anyway."

"Have you ever seen them?"

"No, but things have happened. I've never told a soul." She lowered her voice. "The Good People don't like being talked about."

"What kind of things?" Gwen whispered.

"Ach, well, you could put it down to coincidence

or fancy. Little things. Sometimes breaches in the walls are mended in the night. And once I lost a ewe, and her with a lamb inside her. I was worried sick. Searched everywhere. It was nearly dark and I was almost at the top of Slieve Carron and still no sign of her, when I heard music. A sweet piping sound high up in the air, beckoning to me. I followed after it and it led me right to her. Maybe it's all in the head, but I believe it."

"You're the kind of person they would help."

"And how would you know that?"

A hush had fallen over the two. Both had reached the point where secrets could be aired without judgement or disbelief.

Gwen told her entire story to date, leaving out nothing. After describing the calamity at the banquet, she finished dismally.

"I've screwed everything up. I haven't a clue how to find them again. And I've got to get to Findabhair. She can't stay in Fairyland no matter how much she loves it. This isn't a game. I mean, what am I supposed to tell her parents? She has to come home."

Katie had listened in rapt silence throughout, eyes huge with amazement. She rummaged in her pockets for a cigarette and lit it hurriedly.

"Sorry for polluting your air but I can't manage this without a fag. Bigod what an adventure! You've got a handful there all right."

By this time Gwen was out of bed and dressing herself, but moving slowly as she still felt weak.

"I'll make you a big fry for your breakfast," Katie offered.

"Ugh no. The thought of food makes me ill, and that means there's definitely something wrong with me."

"Shouldn't you stay in bed?"

"I can't. I must get after them. They're probably doing this to slow me down, but I won't let them."

"That's the spirit!" Katie said. "What'll we do? Where shall we go?"

Gwen noted the "we" gratefully. Despite her brave words she was wondering if she had the strength to do anything.

"Back to the Ancient Eating Place, I think. Midir might have left some message for me. He helped me before."

"We'll take the motorbike."

"Don't you have work to do? I shouldn't be dragging you into this."

"Mam and the girls are at it. I'm supposed to be looking after you and that's what I'm doing, right?"

As they sped down the road, Gwen was revived by the cool rush of air. The Burren looked worn out and bedraggled after its stormy night. Branches and twigs were scattered everywhere like rubble. The grykes and potholes in the limestone pavements glistened with rainfall. A turlough had risen to flood a field. The hedges dripped water onto the road.

When they reached the ancient circle where

Gwen's fairy tale had begun, their hopes were quashed. Nothing but sodden ground and damp stones.

"I was sure he would leave some sign." Gwen sat down wearily on a dry patch of grass.

Undaunted, Katie continued to scout the area, but she too had to finally admit it was deserted. She sat down beside her friend, trying to think what they should do next.

"This is hopeless," sighed Gwen. "How to find a fairy in a haystack."

"Ssh," said Katie suddenly. "I hear something."

The two girls went utterly still. The sounds came from behind them. Slowly they turned to face a hedge-row. Nothing could be seen through the tangle of hazel brush, but the noises echoed from the other side. A low crunching munching, accompanied by little sighs and snorts.

Katie laughed under her breath and was about to stand up to see whose goats had strayed, when the voices began. Gwen grabbed her arm and the two sat frozen, hardly believing their ears.

"She made a right hames of the feast last night."

"Bejapers and she did. Ruptions and ructions to beat the band. The place nearly burst asunder."

"There'll be talk of it for ages to come."

"That's what they get for letting that sort into the manor house."

"Ah, but sure they're not all bad. What about our Katie?"

"Our good neighbour?"

"The best there is."

"She's a friend of your one, you know."

"She is that."

"Wants us to lend her a hand and all."

"Oh aye. And we'd have the wrath of the Boss down about our ears before you could say 'tashay mahogany gaspipes.' "

"He'd leave us as we are for another hundred years."

"Ah now, he'd get over it."

"He wouldn't."

"He would."

"He wouldn't."

"He would."

"And he would not."

"Well, who then is going to tell the *gersha* that the court has upped and gone to Boyle?"

"Boyle in the County of Roscommon?"

"Sure who would tell her that?"

"Not me."

"Me neither."

"But she might overhear us, and if she did, I'm thinking, bedad, it wouldn't be our fault now would it?"

"Not at all. Not at all. We couldn't be held accountable if the likes of them takes to eavesdropping."

When the voices fell silent, Katie uttered a little cry and made a dash for her bike. Gwen followed quickly, and with a roaring start, they fled away. Only when she had put a safe distance between herself and the eating place did Katie stop to have a look.

Behind the hedgerow, a herd of wild goats were grazing peacefully.

"Lord God above," she swore softly.

"Scary, isn't it?"

Gwen could see how tightly Katie gripped the handlebars and she understood. The first encounter was definitely the worst.

When they reached the farmhouse, Katie was still too dazed to talk. Gwen sat her on the sofa and made some tea, then went to pack. She consulted her map and found the town of Boyle, though at first she had been looking for a place called "Boil." When she returned to the living room, Katie was near the window, gazing out at the mountains.

"I'm off, Katie. I'm sure you know why. Thanks so much for everything. Especially this. You heard what they said. If it wasn't for you they wouldn't have helped me."

"No, no. Thank *you*, Gwen!"

Katie's eyes shone with a startling light. Now that the initial terror of the unknown had subsided, in its wake brimmed an irrepressible delight and awe.

Gwen could see how she herself must have appeared to Mattie and decided "touched" wasn't so bad after all.

"You can't know what this means to me." Katie's voice shook with emotion. "To know that they are really and truly here. Sometimes I wonder why I bother to keep going. There's so much work to do and never enough hands to do it. You build a wall, it falls down. You tend your cattle day in and day out, then one of them contracts TB and you can't sell any. You sit up all night with a sick lamb and she dies in the morning. And this year's been the worst of all, with Da in the hospital and us not knowing if he'll get well."

"Oh Katie," Gwen said. "I'm so sorry."

Only now did she realize how much harder things were for this girl than for her.

Katie waved away Gwen's sympathy and held her head proudly. "That's life. And that's farming. Nobody said it would be easy. I love it and I wouldn't want to do anything else. But sometimes you need something to keep you going. A dream, or a vision of the future maybe. The fairies have always been my secret comfort." Katie looked out the window. "And they called me their good neighbour!"

Gwen could only smile at Katie's joy. "They know a good thing when they see it."

"I want to come with you."

"You can't. No way. I've already got one to haul out of Fairyland. I'm not going for two."

Katie looked wistful, but she recognized the sense of Gwen's words.

"You're right. I'd never come back. But promise me this. I said it before and I'll say it again. If you need my help, you're to call on me. All right?" Katie spat on her hand and held it out. "Make it a deal, like a true farmer."

Laughing, Gwen spat too, and they shook on the agreement.

"I'll drive you to the main road. Do you know where you're going?"

"Not really. But that hasn't stopped me so far."

CHAPTER FIFTEEN

"Here you are now—this is Boyle."

The truck driver stopped his huge vehicle on a narrow street.

"Sorry, what did you say?" Gwen asked suddenly.

It had happened again! One minute she was sitting there talking to the driver, the next she found herself in a grassy place, blinded by sunlight. From all around came the sounds of laughter and high-pitched voices.

"It's Boyle you want, isn't it?" said the truck driver.

"Oh, yes. Yes. Thank you."

Gwen climbed down from the high cab and looked around in confusion. The town followed the contours of the hills. Houses, shops and pubs creeped up and down the road. At the centre was a stone bridge overlooking a river. She leaned on the bridge to watch the flow of the waters. Why had she come here?

The day had been a blur of faces and places. It hadn't been easy keeping herself on track. Images of the banquet hall would float through her mind, and sometimes she felt as if she were there again. Other times her ears throbbed with fairy music. The worst was the sudden shift of scene, when she found herself somewhere else entirely, somewhere impossibly bright and shining. If it hadn't been for the vagueness that muffled her, Gwen would have been worried. But she was like a leaf drifting downstream, drawn inexorably by some invisible current.

On the outskirts of Boyle, she came upon the ruins of a medieval monastery. The pale grey walls were bordered by trim lawns. Inside, the sky was the roof, a shining canopy of blue, and the cloister was smoothly carpeted with grass. Soft breezes blew through the lancet windows. To her left was a nave, grandiose and airy, lined with vaults and columns that led to a church tower.

Gwen shielded her eyes with her hand. The glare of sunlight on stone made her blink. She felt dizzy. Bells rang out and she could hear voices lifting in song. Her sight began to waver. Where the sky shone above, suddenly a wooden-beamed ceiling ranged overhead. Now she was aware of ghostly figures passing by. Monks in grey tunics padded silently through the corridors, arms folded in wide sleeves and heads bent in prayer.

Gwen ran to the entrance and looked back at the town. It was blurring too, as if veiled by the ripples of a heat wave. The modern buildings would fade and reappear, sometimes replaced by smaller structures with thatched roofs and smoking chimneys. Carts with donkeys and horses moved obliviously through the traffic. People in homespun cloth and bare feet mingled with those in present-day clothing.

"What's happening to me?"

But even the question wasn't clear in Gwen's mind. She felt like a ghost herself, pale and insubstantial. Not quite there, not quite anywhere. And because the feeling wasn't unpleasant, it was difficult to fight. Like the gentle persistence of much-needed sleep, it nudged her slowly but steadily toward surrender. She sat down on the steps of the cloister walk and closed her eyes.

Slumped in a doze, resting peacefully, Gwen was surprised to be roughly shaken awake. Startled, she looked up at the young monk who bent over her.

"Get thee hence, maiden," he whispered urgently. "Be quick before they catch sight of thee. If one of the *Manaigh Liath* even touches thee, thou art trapped in this time."

"What?" cried Gwen and she was up in an instant.

Her eyes confirmed the monk's warning. No longer a ruin, the monastery stood as it had in the Middle Ages. Fully roofed and walled, except for the open cloister, it resounded with the noise of habitation: footsteps, voices and the chime of bells. While the choir of the Grey Monks echoed from the church, the lay brethren laboured at their chores, carrying pails of water and armloads of wood. Smells of baking wafted from the kitchen ovens.

Gwen had no time to recover from her shock. A cry went up as the abbot himself stepped from the rectory and spotted her.

"A woman in the cloister!"

It was only a short dash to the entranceway, but for Gwen it seemed miles. The clamour spurred her on. From every quarter, monks came running and shouting. One reached out to grasp her just before the gate, and her heart sank. All was lost. Then she saw it was the monk who had woken her. With a sharp pull he hauled her over the threshold.

"Go into town," he said hurriedly. "To the House of the Little Branch. You will see the sign." Then he was gone.

It was as if a door had been shut behind her. The noisy pursuit ended abruptly and Boyle Abbey was a ruin once more.

Shaken, Gwen paused to catch her breath. Things were getting serious. She had no doubt she had just narrowly escaped a trap. The young man had been no monk. Under his cowl she had spied the red hair and recognized Midir, her champion in the fairy world. But would the King really imprison her in another time? She shuddered as she remembered her cousin's words. *They can get away with murder without batting an eyelid.* Could the game become deadly? It was more important than ever that she find Findabhair.

"The House of the Little Branch," she muttered to herself, as she went back into town. "Doesn't sound like anything in modern Ireland. And how will I recognize the sign he mentioned?"

At the top of the town, past the clock tower, Gwen found what she was looking for. A wooden placard hung above the door of a public house, creaking gently in the evening breeze. AN CRAOIBHÍN. Though she couldn't translate the Irish name, the painting on the sign was enough to convince her: a fey-looking image of a wooded grove.

She had to grin. "It's a house of sorts and he meant a real sign. Here I was looking for something mystical. Will I ever figure these guys out?"

As she swung open the door of the pub, a blast of music greeted her. A *seisiún* was in progress and the place was packed. Tourists and local people sat together at tables laden with whiskey and stout. In a half circle near the bar, as if onstage, were musicians playing traditional music.

Their virtuosity was dazzling. The tin whistle trilled like birds scattered in flight. The *bodhrán* drum rumbled like peals of thunder. The elbow pipes were a skirl of sound as if a hive of bees sang in tenor and bass. But it was the fiddler who was the most thrilling of all. His bow skipped over taut strings like a stone skimming water. As the audience tried to follow the wild notes, he seemed to pull them along in a frenzied dance—up mountains, down glens and across rushing rivers till they were breathless and exhausted with over-excitement.

When the madcap tune ended with a dashing leap, everyone roared their approval and shouted for more. They had never heard the like of such music.

Now the musicians started up a slow ballad and the singer cleared her throat to begin. Her hand rested on the knee of the fiddle player beside her.

I have left my home and kin behind,
To run away with a dark gypsy king.

Gwen was struggling to get a grip on reality. She didn't know what to make of this cosy little tableau. They all wore blue jeans and T-shirts. Except for the striking good looks and the shining eyes, they appeared no different from any other group of young people. Everyone in the pub accepted them as normal, though wonderfully gifted, musicians. Only Gwen was aware of the truth, that these were not human but fairy folk.

And there was Findabhair blithely singing away, her hand on the denimed knee of the King of the Fairies!

And we dance in the moonlit woods of Sheegara.

Gwen tried to approach them but it was impossible. A wall of bodies, as impenetrable as a rampart, blocked her way. A French couple whose knapsacks were on the floor beside them, made room for her to sit on the bench against the back wall. She sank down in her seat, keeping her eyes on her cousin. Why did Findabhair act as if she didn't see her? She must have spotted Gwen when she entered the pub. What was going on? And she was certainly singing with great emotion for someone who always said she hated folk music. Gwen sat up, all attention. Was this a signal? Was Findabhair trying to tell her something?

You'll find me dancing by the moonlight
At the heart of the woods of old Sheegara.

The fiddler, who was Finvarra, suddenly raised his hand to stop the music. With a wry glance at Findabhair he declared the session over. Despite the cries of dismay and calls for more, the musicians packed up their gear with astonishing speed and exited the pub in a whirlwind of motion.

The audience sat stunned as if they didn't know what hit them. The publican collapsed in his chair and mopped his brow. He never got a crowd at suppertime and had been caught off guard without his barman.

"The Irish are peculiar, *non*?" said the French girl to Gwen.

"*Oui*," she agreed, "*mais c'est la vie.*"

Unlike the others, Gwen wasn't disturbed by the band's hasty departure. She had picked up her cousin's message loud and clear. Now all she had to do was find *Sheegara*.

CHAPTER SIXTEEN

ENQUIRING ABOUT A
tourist information office, Gwen was directed to
another little pub in the town. But none of the scenic
maps or pamphlets on display there made any refer-
ence to Sheegara. The proprietor behind the bar had
never heard of the place, nor had his wife who was
working in the kitchen.

Gwen was beginning to wonder if she had heard
Findabhair right, when an old man, hunched over his
drink in the corner, piped up in a querulous voice,
"Sure none of ye would know the old place-names
any more. They're all dead and buried with the rest of
old Ireland. Gone like the black bicycles that used to
lean against the hedgerows. Gone with the dancing at
the crossroads and the bottled porter."

"Never mind the sermon, Bernie," the barman
said. "Tell the girl where it is, if you know, and I'm sure

that you do." He winked at Gwen. "If it's local history you want, he's your man."

"Sheegara," Bernie said, with maddening slowness. He took a sup of his pint and licked the cream from his lips. "It's the anglified pronouncement for the townland of *Sídhe Gáire*, the home of the 'laughing fairies.' "

"That's it!" Gwen cried. "Can you tell me where?"

"I can. Go out the town apace, past the old abbey, and on up the Sligo road. Take the first turn to your right and you're heading straight for it. Where is it in the townland you might be going?"

"A wood?" Gwen said uncertainly.

The old man's eyes flashed.

"There's new trees up there planted by the Forestry and making a ruination of the land. Is it them you're after?"

"I don't know. How many forests are there?"

"There be old ones that are a thing of beauty, a home for wild creatures and a joy to walk in. Then there be new ones, grown for money, in thin straight lines ready for the chop. It's blood money, I tell ye, that turns good pasture into a wasteland."

"I'm sure they wouldn't approve of that," Gwen said, thinking out loud. "It must be an old one."

Though the publican gave her an odd look, Bernie sensed he had found a kindred soul. His smile was benevolent as he regarded her.

"Long before your time, *gersha*, there was talk of an

ancient woods up there. The Forest of the Red Fairies it was called, and they say it was an enchanted place. You'd want to put your best foot forward if you're looking for it. It'd be twilight before ye find it, I'm thinking."

"The right time for the right place," Gwen murmured.

The proprietor was now looking thoroughly lost, but the old man's eyes twinkled as Gwen thanked him profusely.

"Good luck and God bless," said Bernie as she left the pub.

Following his directions, Gwen walked out of the town, wondering briefly to herself if the old man's hair had been red in his youth. She shuddered when she came in sight of Boyle Abbey but hurried past it onto the Sligo road. She was feeling confident and proud of herself. Despite their tricks, she was still hot on the heels of the fairy court.

"I'm not a bad detective," she told herself. "Nancy Drew and the Case of the Missing Fairies."

Her newfound confidence helped to offset the fact that she felt physically weak and sometimes groggy. She hadn't eaten a meal since the fairy banquet, but the idea of food was strangely revolting. Somewhere in the back of her mind this worried her. Gwen knew the dangers of fasting and would never do it.

I must have a stomach bug, she told herself.

The Sligo road was busy with traffic, but Gwen

didn't stop to hitchhike, afraid that she might miss the turn she wanted. It wasn't long before she reached it, and she soon found herself walking on a byway less travelled, with no cars or people or houses in sight. Overgrown with hawthorn on either side, the narrow lane twisted and turned like a snake in the grass. Then it began to climb upwards into the hills. All around rolled damp fields of green, with knolls and tussocks of scutch grass and furze. Further still, the landscape dropped below her and a breathtaking view was unveiled: a silver chain of lakes at the throat of blue mountains.

Except for the occasional head of cattle, Gwen was utterly alone in the countryside. At one point she passed a small cottage half-buried in the ditch. The once whitewashed walls were grey with neglect. Tattered lace curtains hung limp and dusty. A vase of dead flowers stood in one of the windows. It meant something, she sensed, but she wasn't sure what. The old man's words echoed through her mind. *Gone with the rest of old Ireland.* How much had this country lost forever? And why?

Gwen felt the melancholy settle over her along with the cool breeze of evening that hinted night. Though there were no signposts, she knew she was in the right place even as she had known it in the Burren. It seemed the fairies favoured secluded or forsaken regions. Were they a beleaguered race holding out in the last patches of countryside? Would the spread of towns and roads eventually push them out altogether?

Were they doomed like so many other wild creatures before the onslaught of man?

Gwen was bowed down with a sorrow that was overwhelming, as if a heavy mantle had been placed on her shoulders. The breeze had become a wind that howled over desolate fields. *Ochone. Ochone.*

She could barely put one foot in front of the other. Why did she feel so burdened with grief? When she spotted a figure on the road ahead of her, she forced herself onwards, anxious to meet another soul.

The old woman who stood in the shadow of the hedgerow was small and stooped. Wisps of smoky grey hair trailed out from under the black shawl that draped her head and shoulders. Her long skirt fell to thick brown boots that were caked with mud. But it was her eyes that caught Gwen, bright as two black beads and full of laughter.

"*Nach breá an lá é, a chailín.* A fine evening for a stroll."

"Is this the townland of Sheegara?" Gwen asked, after exchanging a few pleasantries about the weather.

"Oh aye. The home of *Sídhe Gáire* it is. The laughing fairies are just ahead of you now. There's a forest beyant. New pine hiding old woods. This sweet road and your two fine feet will carry you there."

"Thank you," Gwen said, cheered by the old woman's friendliness.

Was this another helpful fairy encouraging her along the last lap? Or was the old woman simply what she appeared to be, another Irish person in tune with the old ways and times. The mingling of the two races was beginning to baffle Gwen.

"Will you bide here and watch the sun set with me?" the old woman asked. "I've no one for company these long days. They've all left for the town or for Amerikay."

Though she knew she should be going, Gwen felt sorry for the old woman. The evening had turned soft and hazy. A slow sunset was suffusing the sky. The clouds were tinted with rose and burnt orange. Below, in the distance, the necklace of lakes reflected the colours like glimmering gems. And rising beyond them, the mountains were aglow with pale purples and blues. It was such a peaceful scene that Gwen chided herself for wanting to leave it. What was the hurry? Time enough for chasing after phantoms. This was real beauty and she should stay and appreciate it.

Gwen had no idea how long she stood there, watching the sky. Nor did she notice the tendrils of the hawthorn as they reached out to catch her. Another gust of wind and the branches clung to her jeans, twining around her legs like climbing ivy. As the briars began to crawl up her arms, the prick of a thorn suddenly broke the spell. With horror Gwen saw that the sun had set and that she was bound hand and limb by brambles.

Trapped again! And so quickly! She had been caught unawares, not expecting another attempt so soon. Didn't Findabhair warn her not to under-estimate the King? *He's a tricky divil.* Furious at herself, as well as the fairies, Gwen struggled against her bonds but to no avail.

"Let go of me!" she screamed in panic at the old woman.

But the decoy herself had been drawn into the hedge. The woman's wrinkled brown skin was the knotted bark of branches. Her skirt and shawl were a mass of leaves. The two bright eyes were ripened berries.

Gwen was shouting at a bush.

That was the last straw. Her fury exploded. With their pranks and their magic, the fairies were literally driving her insane.

"That's it! I've had it!" she roared again.

Now she wrestled the hawthorn with the strength of rage. Leaves flew in the air. She clawed at the brambles and hit back at thorns. Though her knapsack impeded her, she finally freed her arms, and then her legs and she came out kicking. With a final stomp she broke away and raced up the road.

"Just wait till I get them. They've got one angry Canuck on their hands!"

CHAPTER SEVENTEEN

GWEN'S ANGER SPURRED
her onwards, and she didn't stop till the road itself came
to an end. In front of her was a ranch-style wooden
gate. Beyond it ranged a plantation of young pine. The
trees stood to attention just as Bernie had described, row
after row, like soldiers about to be hewn down. Gwen
climbed over the gate and plunged into the forest.
Evening was closing fast. Dusk muted the sky. Somewhere inside this new growth was the old woods of
Sheegara and she had to find it before dark set in.

The scent of pine perfumed the air. Needles and
small cones crunched underfoot. Like Little Red
Riding Hood, trying not to think about wolves, Gwen
wandered deeper and deeper into the forest. At last the
man-made lines of trees gave way to a natural disorder.
Green fern curled at the roots of gnarled oak. Garlands
of ivy clung to lithe beech and wild apple trees. The

ground was soft with moss. Leaves shed dappled light into the air rich with the musty smell of earth.

Something in the woods instilled peace in Gwen. Though night was settling over all like a thick dark blanket, she wasn't afraid. Moonlight quivered through the branches like threads of silver.

Then she heard the music.

High piping notes like the trill of a nightingale. They beckoned to her. Heart beating faster, she crept through the trees. Ahead shone an amber light as if the sun had set in the forest and was burning there. Closer she drew, hiding in the underbrush. As she peeped out from the shelter of leaves, her eyes opened wide with delight. Only now, when she saw them again, did Gwen admit she had been longing for them.

There in a moonlit forest glade, around a bright bonfire, danced the fairies. Flitting and flickering like flames themselves, they footed lightly with unruly glee. Whirling dervishes and spinning tops would be slow beside them. They capered in giddy circles like leaves caught in eddies of wind.

Gwen couldn't tell if they were tall or tiny. Their clothes were flower petals and puffs of thistledown, yet they also seemed to shadow the trees. Holly berries were strewn in hair brown as the branches. Apples dangled like earrings from scalloped ears. Whereas they had been silver-hued against the Burren's moonlit stones, here they were of a darker colouring, russet brown, apple-red, dark-green and ruddy. Were they chameleons? Camouflaged by their surroundings? Was their glamour in the fairy hall yet another guise?

Suddenly a dark form leaped over the bonfire and scattered the fairies with the screech of a hawk. In command of the clearing, he began to dance with a breathtaking perfection of grace and control. Vivid colours gleamed on his body like paint. His dark eyes were scrolled with blue designs. The long hair was sleek and black as a panther's. He would move slowly, like a dream, then change to quick fluttering motions, the tilt of his head or the crook of an arm. Even the eyes flitted and flicked—and the fingers and the toes— as if he were dance itself in every fibre of his being. And on his brow was a glittering star. Finvarra, the King, Lord of the Dance.

"Isn't he beautiful?"

The husky whisper took Gwen by surprise, and she almost stumbled from her hiding place. Her face flushed hot in the cool night air.

"Don't speak," Findabhair warned as she caught hold of Gwen. Then she led her deeper into the forest.

They came to the ruins of an old stone wall that had once enclosed an apple orchard. The apple trees had long since run wild and were overgrown with weeds and ivy. Gwen followed her cousin along the wall till they reached a little grotto built over a well. The water shone in the moonlight like a pool of silver. Findabhair stood on one side of the well and positioned Gwen on the other.

"We can talk normally now," she said out loud. "They can't hear voices that cross over water. Am I ever glad to see you, Gwen! I've been mad with worry. You're in terrible trouble. Are you feeling all right?"

Gwen was too surprised to speak at first. She was stunned by her cousin's appearance. Like the fairies, Findabhair had also changed. She was dressed in her own clothes, the ones she'd worn in the pub in Boyle, but they were shredded in ribbons and interlaced with moss. Her feet and arms were bare, her skin nut-brown. A daisy chain crowned her hair, which stood out like a bush, matted with leaves. She looked beautiful in a wild fierce way, but the eyes were too bright, too wild.

"Let's get going," Gwen urged. "I'm here to help you escape."

The peal of laughter was like a blow. "Help me? You're the one who needs help."

Gwen was speechless. Was this really her cousin? Was she under a spell? But now Findabhair stopped laughing and her look was serious. She seemed to change her moods as quickly as the fairies.

"Don't you know what has happened, Gwen? Can't you recognize the signs? Have you eaten any food since the fairy banquet? Are you finding it hard to keep a grip on where you are?"

Gwen nodded reluctantly.

"You're half in, half out. That was the judgement by the time the row was settled. Your body dwells amongst mortals but your spirit is in Fairyland. You're being pushed and pulled between the two. You'll keep falling into the cracks, through time and different worlds. It can only get worse."

Gwen's blood ran cold, not only because of her cousin's words but the way she'd said them. So calmly and coolly.

"You're not Findabhair," she accused her. "You're a changeling, like in the stories, a fairy pretending to be human."

Findabhair shook her head. The sympathy in her eyes was the worst blow of all. Gwen so needed to believe this wasn't her cousin.

"I know they're affecting me," Findabhair said quietly, "but I haven't changed that much. I was never one to mince my words. I'm telling you the truth for your own sake. So you can save yourself. There's no danger to me. I've chosen to join them. If you would only do the same, everything would be fine!"

"This is crazy!" Gwen said, suddenly afraid.

Everything was upside down. Up till now, as far as Gwen was concerned, both the danger and the decision about Fairyland were Findabhair's. Not hers! She wasn't prepared for this reversal. The fairies had pulled the rug out from under her feet. And to add to her upset was the secret clamour inside, the quietly insidious urge to say yes.

"We can't just take off like this," she argued frantically, as much with herself as with Findabhair. "What about our parents, our friends, our lives? We were born to be human, not to be fairies. You've got to stop this and stop it now. It's crazy, I'm telling you."

"Crazy?"

Findabhair's tone was a mixture of amusement and impatience. The familiar I-know-better-than-you look confirmed once and for all that she was no imposter.

"Gwen, this is what you and I have been searching for since we were kids. All our secret hopes and dreams. Here they are on a silver platter and you're refusing them. Who, I ask you, is the madwoman here?"

Gwen's head was swirling. It wasn't fair. This wasn't the kind of choice one should have to make in a lifetime. She had never thought it would come to this. The battle raged within, one side crying out to join the fairies, the other quietly refusing to forsake her own world.

Findabhair could see her confusion and spoke persuasively. "I love my ordinary life too, but it's not as if I'll never see it again. I phoned Mum from town, by the way, and told her we're having a great time. Gwen, everything is possible when you're a magical being."

"That's not true," Gwen argued, "and you know it isn't. You can't have your cake and eat it too. You can't live in both worlds at the same time. You're only a visitor to our world now. You don't live here any more."

"Midir fancies you, you know," Findabhair said, changing her tactics. "We could be queens together. Just imagine the crack!"

"I'm too young to get married!" Gwen shouted, furious with her cousin. It was bad enough trying to sort out the situation; she didn't need a handsome young man being dangled as bait. "And so are you, Findabhair Folan! And neither you nor that boyfriend of yours is going to boss me around or trick me into doing something I haven't decided for myself. And that's that!"

Findabhair was taken aback by the force of Gwen's speech. "I'm not the only one who has changed, cuz."

The admiration in her voice calmed Gwen down. A thoughtful silence fell between the two. Their long friendship rose up like a fire to warm them, reminding each how much they liked the other.

"Why don't these guys go for fairy women?" Gwen's tone was lighter. "I mean, aside from the fact that we're beautiful and intelligent, what's the attraction?"

Findabhair laughed. "Novelty, my dear. These people have been alive for aeons. They know each other so well they'd die of boredom if it wasn't for us. Humans, I mean. Could you imagine a marriage lasting for a thousand years? Then multiply that by a few thousand more."

"I see your point." Gwen sighed. "I don't know if this is a dream or a nightmare."

She had barely uttered her words when a blast of wind shook the trees around them. The fairy folk had arrived. Dressed in tatters, they were like ragged children, with faces smudged and hair tangled with ivy.

The King stepped forward to catch hold of Findabhair. Gwen felt as if she were surrounded by a band of
outlaws led by Maid Marian and Robin Hood.

Finvarra bowed courteously to Gwen. His voice
was cool and dark like an underwater stream.

"Thou hast free will in this matter and thou hast
not. Death is one of the penalties for those who come
unbidden to us, but we grant thee life instead. Our life.
To sleep in a mound is to place oneself under the sway
of Faërie. Yet we were kind and did yield to thy choice
not to come with us. Thou didst pursue us and entered
into our court. In sporting spirit we tempted thee.
Thou wert warned not to eat of our food yet thou
didst eat. The judgement is fair, the decision is thine.
Accept our rightful claim to thee or be banished forever, a shadow in your own land.

"What dost thou say?"

CHAPTER EIGHTEEN

G WEN WAS THINKING
fast. How was she going to get out of this one? Even
she had to admit there was a strong case against her.
Findabhair's eyes pleaded while Midir hovered nearby
with a hopeful look.

"I'm not saying yes and I'm not saying no," she
began, then finished hurriedly as the King's eyes
flashed. "I need to think about it. If you own eternity,
what's a little time?"

True to his nature, Finvarra's quick temper
changed to delight. A smile of approval brightened his
features. "You wish to continue the game?"

Gwen nodded and held her breath as he considered the proposal. "It has been good sport thus far."

With a royal wave of his hand, he made his decision. "Granted. A little time. No more than a day of
your own reckoning. We go to our northern kingdom

by the Lake of Shadows. Join us there tomorrow's eve or accept your doom."

"Where?" Gwen asked him, happy to have gained this much. "I don't know Ireland very well."

Findabhair was about to answer, but the King cut her off. "In your world it is called—" he paused, eyes sparkling with mischief "—island island."

The fairy troop burst into laughter and again Findabhair tried to speak, but in the blink of an eye they were gone. Gwen stood alone in the forest night.

"Island island. Now what's that supposed to mean? Trickster to the last. But I've found them before, I'll find them again."

Gwen looked around for a good spot to camp down for the night. Heaping leaves against the shelter of the old stone wall, she spread out her sleeping bag. The moonlight was bright enough to see by, but she kept her flashlight handy in case she got frightened. And yet, she realized, marvelling at herself, she wasn't afraid.

"All in a day's work." She grinned tiredly, as her eyes closed.

It was in the deep of night she awoke. Emerging from the warm dark bath of sleep, she found herself drifting upwards like thistledown on the breeze. Or was she a butterfly newly risen from her cocoon? She felt impossibly tiny, like a speck of starlight. A sudden shift in the wind sent her tumbling. Now she was caught in an eddy and spun madly around. The whirl of dust and leaves made her dizzy with laughter.

Am I a fairy? she wondered.

And she suddenly felt, with an ache of joy, the leaf-thin pale-veined wings that fluttered from her shoulders.

"Gwenhyvar! Come dance with us!"

The voices echoed from everywhere. She was not only surrounded by others of her kind—tiny, winged and light as air—but by every creature and spirit who lived in the forest. Nocturnal insects, birds and animals sang in chorus as the night quivered with the swift movements of elemental beings. Wood nymphs and dryads encircled their trees, tossing leaves like confetti. Sylphs of the air clasped groups of fairies as if gathering up armfuls of flowers. Anyone or anything awake in the night was part of the song and caught up in the dance.

As easily as making a daisy chain, Gwen intertwined herself amongst the dancers. Arm to branch, catch petal and wing, hand to paw, here's antenna and tail! In the shadow of the forest, beneath the sky of stars, it all seemed so simple. This dance had begun in ancient days and would continue on throughout eternity. All that belonged to life danced this dance together.

Gwen awoke early the next morning to the sound of birds. Sunlight streamed onto her face through the branches of the apple tree that hung above her head like a canopy of green lace. The last images of a wonderful dream trailed away with the night but left her happy. She jumped out of her sleeping bag, stripped off her clothes and washed herself with the icy water of the well. The shock of cold made her whoop out loud, and she danced on the forest floor to dry herself off.

"I'm going fairy." She laughed, tucking leaves in her hair.

Despite the ultimatum hanging over her, she had to admit she was feeling on top of the world. No matter how many obstacles they put in her path, they had yet to defeat her. She knew in a way she had never known before that she was strong and independent and capable of anything.

As Gwen walked back through the forest to reach the road, she found herself smiling at everything as if they were old friends. Why did that clump of mushrooms look so familiar? She suddenly saw herself perched on one, sharing a cup of nectar with a lively fieldmouse. And that twisted bit of root and tree stump looked amazingly like a statue of Pan; the face bent toward the flute of a twig, the green moss was the hair of a satyr's limb. Gwen grinned at her own imaginings and hurried on. Behind her piped a trill of music.

Once on the road, she marched past the spot where the old fairy woman had tried to trap her. With a jaunty toss of her head, she saluted the bush. And when she came to the ruined abbey of Boyle, she admired its grandness without trepidation.

The town itself was just waking up for the day.

Delivery vans pulled in at butcher's, baker's and grocery shops. Ale barrels were rolled into the cellars of pubs with a great rumble and clatter of metal. Doors opened to usher people out to work, their sleepy faces lighting up at the welcome sunshine. Gwen entered the pub–cum–tourist office where she hoped to find Bernie, but it was obviously too early. The proprietor was polishing glasses behind the empty bar.

"Excuse me. Is there a place in the north of Ireland called 'island island'?"

Gwen could tell by his look that he was beginning to wonder about her. Then his face brightened.

"This is for the cryptic crossword in the *Irish Times*, is it?"

"Yeah," she replied, though she had no idea what he was talking about.

He screwed up his face with concentration, then went into the kitchen to question his wife. He returned in triumph.

"Inch Island, County Donegal," he declared. "'Inch' is an English derivation of *Inish*, which is 'island' in Irish. Inch Island. Island island. How's that for you? The wife has brains to burn."

"Great. Thanks," said Gwen. After a moment's pause, she threw all pretence to the wind. "How do I get there?"

CHAPTER NINETEEN

‹‹

WITH MOST OF THE DAY
spent travelling and changing buses, Gwen arrived in
the early evening at the village of Burnfoot. The single
unpaved street with its inn, café, shop and post office
was deserted. All around rose the green and brown hills
of Donegal. The rain-damp air had a freshness that
hinted of the northern sea nearby. Gwen went into the
shop to ask directions for Inch Island.

"No, you won't be needing a boat," she was told
good-humouredly. "There's a causeway to the island as
fine as any road. You might have to walk it, though,
unless a car passes you by. First left outside the village,
go along a winding road, then left again and you're on
the causeway."

"Is there a place to stay on the island?"

"Oh aye. The Clan House of the O'Dohertys
takes in visitors. It's run by an American like yourself."

"Canadian," Gwen said automatically, though she was already out the door.

Outside the village, she was met by a little boy on a tricycle. The impish face grinned up at her from beneath a mop of dark curls. His eyes were big and bright with mischief. He held out his hand to proffer an apple, dark-red and shining.

"Oh thank you! How sweet of you."

It was the first thing Gwen felt like eating in ages. As she bit into the crisp fruit, the child let out a crow of delight.

"Tonight you will play with me on the Plain of the Apple Trees."

Gwen dropped the apple as if it had a worm. "What did you say?"

But the boy was already speeding away, legs pedalling with all the urgency of childhood. She stared after him, bewildered. Was he just a little kid talking about an orchard? Or was he a fairy child trying to lure her into a trap? The collision of worlds was taking its toll. She was finding it hard to know what was real and what wasn't. Everyone and everything was becoming suspect.

"Wow, I'm really getting paranoid."

But something *had* happened.

Gwen grew aware of it as she trudged down the road. She was finding it difficult to breathe. The dense growth of bushes lining the way pressed in against her. Her movements slowed as if she were wading through water. The knapsack dragged on her shoulders like a bag of bricks. It felt like forever before she reached the causeway.

When she stepped onto the causeway that joined Inch to the mainland, Gwen suddenly picked up. A breeze blew over the water to refresh her. Swans glided on the cool green surface. In the distance rose the shadow of the Donegal mountains, shrouded in the purple haze of twilight. Her eyes settled on the cashel that crowned a high hill. The Grianán of Aileach, an ancient stone fort. Once she would have wanted to see it, but now she looked upon it with a cold eye. Would she make her last stand within those walls?

Her strategy was prepared. She had worked out the details on her long journey north. A speech about freedom of choice to appeal to the fairies' good nature and sense of fair play. Then the offer of possible compromises. Finally, a last-ditch attempt to escape, hopefully with Midir's help, dragging Findabhair along whether she liked it or not.

I'll do it. I can do it, she told herself.

Gwen walked smartly across the causeway, but as soon as she set foot on the other side she was overwhelmed by weakness once more. Didn't Findabhair say something about the fairies having less power near water? Were they jinxing her somehow? After the brief feeling of wellbeing as she'd crossed the causeway, the return of whatever it was seemed even worse. Her feet felt as if they were encased in cement.

Though she used all her will-power to keep in motion, Gwen didn't get far on the island road. When her knees buckled under her, she couldn't stop herself from falling. As she lay on the road struggling vainly to get up, a cyclist came speeding around the corner. He skidded to a stop as soon as he saw her, but lost control of his bike and toppled over with a crash.

"Jesus, Mary and Joseph. What the—"

The cyclist swore vociferously as he extricated himself from the tangle of wheels and handlebars. Then he realized that Gwen was still slumped on the road. "Good God, did I hit you?"

Gwen stared helplessly up at the handsome young man. He had nut-brown hair and startling green eyes. She couldn't move her lips to speak. He got her to her feet, but her legs were like rubber and she collapsed again. Frantically he searched her head and limbs for some hidden wound.

It was such an absurd situation that Gwen would have laughed if she could. Somehow the fairies had turned her into a rag doll. Though her mind was clear, she had no control whatsoever over her body. And here was this boy her own age, almost crazy with worry and she couldn't tell him.

"I'm taking you to Granny's," he decided suddenly. "She'll know what to do."

Removing Gwen's knapsack, he put it in the bushes along with his bike. Then he hoisted her up in a fireman's carry and set off quickly down the road.

Hedges of purple-red fuchsia, grey stone walls and fields of green trailed past Gwen's line of vision at a sideways tilt. Feeling like a sack of potatoes, she worried that she might be too heavy to carry. But the young man's broad back bore her easily, and she could sense the strength in his shoulders and arms.

When they reached a small cottage bordered by a wild and profuse garden, he put her down. The door was opened by a grey-haired woman, tall and regal-looking, with keen dark eyes. She wore faded dungarees over a short-sleeved blouse. Her arms were brown and mottled from the sun. The dark eyes narrowed when she saw they were in trouble.

"What have you brought us, Dara?" she said quietly.

She helped him bring Gwen into the house, where they laid her on a sofa bed in the kitchen. Dara described the accident, explaining that he was sure he hadn't struck her. Granny checked Gwen over and declared nothing broken, then stared for a long time into her eyes.

"It's some kind of shock," Dara said. "She's a tourist, I think. There's a Canadian flag on her haversack. I left it by the road with my pushbike. Shall I go and get it? It might tell us who she is."

Gwen was beginning to feel the first inkling of terror. No matter how hard she tried, she couldn't communicate with them.

Granny saw the fear and laid a cool hand on her brow. "You'll be fine, ashy-pet. You're safe with us."

Dara frowned at Granny. "Shouldn't we get a doctor? If she's a foreigner, it might be best if you didn't treat her. This could be a bad business altogether."

Granny shook her head. "No odds where she comes from, medicine won't help her. Not the new kind, anyway. There's a *pishreog* on her—of that I am certain. It wasn't you that struck her but a fairy dart."

Though Dara looked surprised, he didn't argue. It was evident he respected this woman's opinion.

"Go and collect her things and your bike. On your way back, bring me branches from the ash tree and the whitethorn that grows on the Fargan Knowe. Take care as you pass the lone bush on the hill near the hollow. It's a *skeog* and if the fairies are there they will try to hinder you."

"I am the island king, Granny. They would not hinder me."

"Perhaps not. But your kingship will surely be put to the test tonight. They will come for her soon by the looks of things."

Gwen was beginning to wonder if she were hallucinating. Was she putting words into their mouths to suit her predicament? The old lady looked like a retired schoolteacher or librarian. Was she really calling Dara a king? Surely that wasn't possible in present-day Ireland even if one ignored the blue jeans and Sinéad O'Connor T-shirt. Had the fairies finally pushed her over the edge?

When Dara was gone, Granny bent over Gwen, and her face was both stern and kind. "I could bring in a modern doctor, my dear, but it would do you no good. My name is Grania Harte and I am a fairy doctress. I don't expect you to understand; few would recognize my art in this day and age. But you couldn't have gotten into this hubble without having undergone some misadventure with the Wee Folk. There is no one who can help you if I do not."

Well what do you know, Gwen thought to herself. She's a witch.

CHAPTER TWENTY

GRANNY HARTE'S KIT-chen was an odd mixture of old and new. In one corner a refrigerator partnered an electric stove, while the opposite wall was dominated by a fireplace in which hung a black cauldron. Above a floor of shiny linoleum, bunches of herbs dangled from the ceiling amidst strings of onions and dried wildflowers. A portable television was squeezed onto a shelf crammed with crockery jars labelled by hand: *roseroot, eyebright, eglantine, silverweed, groundsel, foxglove.* Behind the door leaned an ancient besom broom, above it a calendar from the Bank of Ireland.

Granny moved about the room with quiet purpose. There was something wolf-like about her; the tall wiry form, the grey hair tied back severely from a pointed face. Though she appeared to be doing domestic tasks, her actions hinted of a secret power.

She lit a fire in the hearth and tossed powders and herbs onto the flames. The air was filled with a musky scent. Then she worked at the stove over a boiling pot, brewing up a concoction that smelled heavy and sweet.

Like a helpless invalid, Gwen could do nothing but watch, yet she was reassured by Granny's quiet confidence. When a cup was placed to her lips, she did her best to swallow the murky liquid. To her surprise it had a pleasant flavour of peppermint and honey and something tart.

"At the heart of this drink," Granny explained, "is the root of the elder tree mingled with yarrow, the herb of seven needs. You'll go into a fever but do not be alarmed. It is to break the hold of fairy influence."

Gwen could feel the drink coursing through her like liquid fire. Her body began to twitch, first with pins and needles, then with aches and pains. She uttered little cries when the jabs grew sharp. Though she knew she was being cured and she tried hard to endure it, tears trickled down her cheeks. She wanted to be home in her own bed, looked after by her mother, not suffering quietly in this house of strangers.

When Dara came in, he stood at the edge of the sofa and looked down at her with sympathy.

"Poor wean," he said. "I would take it for you if I could."

His sea-green eyes were gentle and sincere. As she stared back at him, Gwen felt a little better. Strangers, yes, but good strangers.

"Have you the branches?" Granny asked him.

"Lashins of them. On my pushbike."

"Wreathe the doorway and windows. Then strew this bag of primroses on the threshold and sills. I gathered them on May Eve, so they are very potent. These will keep out the Wee Folk. My only fear is that they will call up something older against which we are powerless."

Dara stood straighter, his voice steady. "Rare are the times my kingship comes into use. I am ready to defend her."

It was dark by the time he had finished his work. Night pressed against the windows like black water. An urgency crept into Granny's preparations. At the four corners of Gwen's bed, she placed a lighted candle, a bowl of salt, a glass beaker of water and a stone of blue chalcedony. Then she and Dara sat on chairs each side of the girl.

"Be of good courage," Granny said gently. "No harm can befall you while I and the king are near."

Gwen's fever was reaching its peak. Though neither Dara nor Granny appeared nervous, the air was taut with tension. The waiting was the worst. What terrible thing might come to collect her?

When the first sounds came it was almost a relief. For better or worse, this was it.

A scampering of feet like a dog at the door. The handle rattled. Muffled cries of dismay. Though nothing was visible, the noises moved to a window. Something tapped on the pane. More angry whispers. Dara and Granny sat without moving. The unseen prowlers circled the cottage, but evidently their way was barred. Whoever or whatever did not enter and the noises faded into the distance.

Dara was about to stand up but Granny shook her head and he remained in his place. It was a few minutes before the next attempt was made. This time the knock on the door was not gentle. After a prolonged battering, a harsh voice cried out, "Open! Open!"

"Who goes there?" Granny called back. "No guests are welcome tonight."

The door burst open and a cold gust of wind hurled itself into the room. Dishes rattled in the cupboard, the curtains flapped wildly and the fire in the grate roared into life.

A giantess stepped into the kitchen. Black gown, black cape and eyes like burning coals. The most terrible thing about her was the horn that protruded from her brow. A creature from the ancient night. The dreadful eyes surveyed the room, glaring first at Granny, then Dara, and finally Gwen on the bed.

"Who are you?" Granny demanded.

"I am the Witch of the One Horn."

The apparition turned away from them and hunched down by the hearth. From her cloak she pulled out a ball of white thread and began to toss it in her hands with violent motions. Then she paused to cry out. "Where are my sisters?"

In response, another giantess entered the room. Dressed the same as the first, she had two horns on her head and whiskers that jutted from her chin like a beard. "Give me place," she screeched. "I am the Witch of the Two Horns."

The second witch had no sooner joined the first when a third came in, bearing three horns like a hideous crown. She too hunched down with her sisters and the three began to enact a strange ritual.

The first unwound the ball of thread and twisted a part of it around her horn. She passed the skein to the second sister, who strung it onto both her horns, then it was passed again to the third, who did likewise to pass it on once more. Against the red flames of the fire they made an eldritch silhouette, three antlered figures threaded together.

Gwen, dimly conscious on the bed, was convinced she was having the worst nightmare of her life.

The witches began to intone, one after the other.

"She was born into this world."

"She is claimed by another."

"Split the thread between the two."

"It is too thin. It will break."

"Then cut it short."

At this point, Granny intervened with a signal to Dara. The two rushed to the fire. Before the witches could move, they had joined the circle and caught up the thread.

In a high voice, Granny proclaimed, "I, Grania

Harte, Wise Woman of Inch, take this thread for my house and hearth."

Dara spoke next. "I, Dara McCrory, King of Inch, claim this thread to be of my land and territories."

A shriek rose up from the witches, and a chorus of howls echoed outside. Then the giantesses fled out the door, their wails ringing through the night like the cries of the banshee.

Dara and Granny stood by the fire, the thread of life still entwined in their hands. Carefully they brought it over to Gwen, who was suffering the last onslaught of fever. As they laid it gently upon her, the thread disappeared and her fever broke. Flooded with peace, she closed her eyes and drifted into a much-needed slumber.

Later Gwen awoke to see two shadows by the fire. After a moment's fright, she realized it was Dara and Granny. They sat together with cups of tea, talking in low voices.

"What will we say to her? She can't possibly understand these matters."

"She must know something, Dara. She has slept on a rath or in a mound. And she had the look of one who has eaten fairy food. She must have gone among them. But the crisis is over and we can question her tomorrow. The truth is always the quickest way. We will not pretend this didn't occur."

Gwen tried to rouse herself. She wanted to join them and talk about all that had happened. She knew she was free from the fairies and in a safe house. But too worn out from the night's trials, she fell back asleep with one worry still on her mind.

What about Findabhair?

CHAPTER TWENTY-ONE

It wasn't only the delicious smell of eggs and bacon that woke Gwen up, but the rumblings of an appetite she hadn't felt for ages. Granny Harte stood at the stove, a flowered apron around her waist. Sunlight was streaming through the open windows. The scene was so cosy and normal that Gwen wondered for a moment if the night's horrors hadn't been caused by her fever. But she knew too much about that other reality to dismiss it so easily.

When Granny turned to check on her, Gwen spoke frankly. "Thank you for saving my life."

The older woman blinked at the straight-forward statement, then smiled broadly. "You're very welcome, my dear. I was just doing my job. If you'd like to freshen up before breakfast, the bathroom is down the hall to your left. Your clothes are in the airing cupboard."

In the washroom, Gwen was a little surprised by the pink enamelled fittings and fluffy towels. What had she expected from a fairy doctress—slugs and snails and puppy dogs' tails? She giggled to herself as she took a shower and changed into clean jeans and a T-shirt. When she returned to the kitchen, Granny set a plate in front of her heaped with bacon, eggs, sausages and fried mushrooms. There was also brown soda bread lathered with butter and a pot of strong tea. Gwen tucked into the feast with gusto.

"My name is Gwen Woods," she said, between mouthfuls. "I owe you an explanation."

"Have your breakfast first, then we can chat. Dara is gathering seaweed for my garden and will join us soon."

When Dara came in, Gwen went suddenly shy. He stood in the doorway to remove his rubber boots, then rolled up his shirtsleeves to wash at the sink. He was very good-looking—she hadn't imagined that. The brown hair fell loosely around finely-honed features. The stare of the sea-green eyes was open and friendly.

"You're looking well," he said, with a slightly crooked grin, as he sat down at the table.

Granny handed him his breakfast. Gwen was glad she had finished hers as she would have been too self-conscious to eat.

"Now, pet," said Granny, as she poured fresh tea and then sat down herself, "perhaps you are ready to tell us how you came to be fairy-struck on Inch Island."

After all they had done for her, Gwen felt she should tell her story from beginning to end. She left out nothing, despite her embarrassment in parts. When she was finished, she waited anxiously for their reaction. She had broken so many rules, made so many mistakes and then brought her problems into their house.

Granny nodded thoughtfully. "Just as I suspected. There was a fairy dart in the apple the little boy gave you. Finvarra was taking no chances you'd be strong enough to fight him. You were holding your own quite nicely till then."

The tone of approval heartened Gwen. She saw the same admiration in Dara's eyes with the added hint of envy. "What an adventure you've been having! And well met, despite the obstacles. You're a great girl altogether."

She blushed at his praise and for the first time was secretly glad that Findabhair wasn't around.

"Does your cousin intend to live permanently with the fairies?"

Gwen detected a note of concern behind Granny's question. "I don't know. We never get much of a chance to talk. Finvarra always separates us. She definitely loves it there, but maybe I can convince her just to stay for the summer and then come home."

Dara and Granny exchanged glances.

"It's not that simple," Dara said. "You can't do as you please with them. There are rules and customs that govern what goes on between us and the Good Folk."

Gwen recognized the echo of Mattie's warning.

"You mean, if she chose to leave they wouldn't let her? Is she really a prisoner?"

Granny sighed. "As Dara says, it's not that simple. The customary length of time for a 'stay' in Fairyland is seven years. This is regardless of choice. Many of our kind have visited the fairies of their own free will, but others have been stolen: young men to take part in their sports and games; new mothers to wet-nurse their babies; beautiful girls to be the King's bride. The marriages are also for seven years but they can be longer if the mortal wishes."

A shadow crossed Granny's face, then she continued. "The fairies bless whoever goes among them with special gifts. Many a famous musician of Ireland has 'gone abroad' to return with the plaintive airs of Faërie. Others are given wonder tales to delight this world or the lore of healing with herbs and plants. If a visit goes badly, if the human tries to trick the fairies or steal their riches, they can be cursed with ill health, bad luck, even sickness unto death."

"Are you saying Findabhair will be there for at least seven years?!"

"It is not such a terrible thing." Granny's look was wistful. "I myself lived among them for that length of time, which is when I acquired my knowledge and arts."

Gwen was wondering how she could possibly explain this to her aunt and uncle. But no, it was too absurd.

"If I can get my cousin to leave earlier, could you free her as you freed me?"

"If she were willing, I could try. But I can't guarantee anything. We'd have to outwit the masters of trickery."

Dara frowned at Granny. "You haven't mentioned the Hunter's—"

"And I won't," Granny broke in. "Not unless it's necessary. We have our hands full as it is. There's no need to add to our worries if it isn't the time. I will cast a fairy calendar today. You two make yourselves a picnic and go for a wander around the island. There are things I must do alone. Show Gwen the shelly beach, Dara, and the old fort and the Cairn. Keep clear of the fairy fort at Dunfinn. If Finvarra is on Inch that's where he'll be.

"Enjoy yourselves now before we take on our task. I have a feeling our troubles have only begun."

CHAPTER TWENTY-TWO

THE NARROW ISLAND ROAD hugged the coastline of Inch. Fields of green and yellow rolled down to the waters of Lough Swilly, which flowed onwards to the northern sea. The mainland was in sight, both to the east and west, the horizon embraced by a ridge of mountains. Brindled slopes of green forest and brown furze were dabbed by strokes of pale grey stone.

"That's Gollan Hill," Dara pointed out, "and the dark one behind is The Scalp. The islanders have a saying, 'When The Scalp puts on her nightcap, Inch may look out.' "

"Meaning?" asked Gwen.

"If there are storm clouds on her summit, we're in for wild weather."

They strolled together along the sunlit road. Picnic

basket under one arm, Dara enthusiastically described everything they passed.

"That green trail leads to Dunfinn, the island's fairy fort. See how it keeps to the left of the whins and bramble? The 'sinister' or left-handed way is always the fairy route. This height ahead of us with the stand of trees is the Fargan Knowe. The windiest spot on the island. There is a name on every part of Inch, it is so well known and loved."

Dara talked easily without shyness or reserve. Gwen was happy just to look and listen. Because he was so attractive, she still felt tongue-tied. But he obviously enjoyed entertaining her and looked pleased whenever he made her laugh. When they reached a level place with a commanding view, Gwen admired the cream-coloured mansion that graced the site.

"Does that belong to the local gentry?"

Dara sputtered with laughter. "Actually, it's the milkman's house."

"Score one for modern Ireland," said Gwen, and she laughed too.

"You have a brilliant laugh," he said.

Now the road plunged downwards, hurrying their legs along till they reached a sandy beach and a pier where fishing boats were moored. Like dolphins, the trawlers gently nosed the dock where nets lay drying in the sun.

"Why didn't I bring my bathing suit?" Gwen groaned.

"Afraid to get wet?"

Before she could defend herself, Dara had dragged her across the sand and into the water. Gwen screeched with laughter. This was no time to be shy. A battle was on. As he tried to dunk her, she flung both arms around his neck to pull him down with her under the waves. After a lot of wrestling and splashing, both emerged, dripping like seaweed, to lie on the shore.

Gwen was still basking in the sun to dry her clothes when Dara called out to her. He had written their names in the sand.

"Shall I put a heart around them?" he asked.

His tone was friendly, his eyes full of mischief. She wasn't sure if he were teasing. Gwen shrugged and gave him a long look. His clothes were drenched and clotted with sand. A crown of sea-wrack was askew on his head. The green and brown strands glistened darkly, like the wet brown hair and the eyes, green as the waves.

"Are you really a king?"

The green eyes flashed. "I am king of this island."

He began to sketch the heart around their names, talking as he worked.

"There are many such kings in Ireland—on Tory, Aran and other islands. It means nothing officially though in some places we have special rights or duties—distributing the post from the mail-boat or opening regattas and patterns."

"Only kings? No queens?"

"Not that I know of. But the kings are through the female line. My uncle, my mother's brother, was king before me. He died in a motor accident. My sister's son will be king after me. As I said, it doesn't mean anything nowadays, but the older generation will acknowledge me in their own way. They give me gifts at Christmas time and once in a while they ask me to mediate if there's a quarrel between neighbours."

He finished the heart and stood with his hands on his hips, to grin at her. "It means much more to the fairy folk. We are the only kings they recognize. They have no time for the *Taoiseach* at all." He started to laugh and at Gwen's puzzled look, explained. "The *Taoiseach* is our elected prime minister. The Good People still follow the old bloodlines."

Gwen was no longer surprised that someone could talk of fairies and prime ministers in the same breath. Nor did she find it hard to consider Dara a king. There was something special about him. But what was she to make of this heart in the sand?

Dara picked up their basket and nodded toward the stone wall by the pier. "I know a great spot for a picnic."

"Isn't this private property?" Gwen said, as they clambered over the wall.

"Yes and no. It's the old fort. Military, not fairy. First built in Napoleon's time and then again in World War I. A New Age Community lives in it now, or so they call themselves. They don't mind visitors."

On the other side of the wall was a grassy demesne with renovated buildings, groves of trees and walled gardens. Children played in front of the houses. Clothes flapped on washing lines. A polytunnel of translucent plastic sheltered a multifarious array of fruits and vegetables.

"They come from all over the world," Dara told her. "Australia, Italy, Germany, North America. Ireland too. The islanders think of them as hippies, but they aren't really. They believe in all kinds of things, including the fairies, but they use computers and other modern technology."

Gwen looked around her. "It's so weird . . . to know that so many people believe . . . But really, Dara, are you telling me most people do?"

Dara laughed. "Irish people, you mean? They do and they don't. Let's face it, what have fairies to do with jobs and politics, new roads or farming? The two worlds have never been so far apart. But you wouldn't find too many country people willing to cut down trees on a fairy fort. Not for love nor money."

They had reached the summit of the old fort where the grass-grown turrets and tunnels brooded over Lough Swilly. The cliffs sheered down below them. Waves crashed against the rocks. Sea birds cried in the air as they dipped and glided. Across the water was a sweep of mountains with the towns of Rathmullan and Buncrana nestled underneath. The wind carried the tang of salt from the ocean beyond.

"So much to think about," Gwen murmured. "Fantasy was always my own little world. I guess I needed it because I was unhappy. But I never thought it could be so real or that so many others shared it too."

Dara stretched out on the grass, resting his head on his arm. Around him was spread the lunch they had brought—home-made bread, chunks of cheese, mandarins and apples. He was watching Gwen as she stared over the mountains.

"I like the way you think. Most girls are only interested in clothes and make-up."

Gwen was quick to retort, "That's not true. Girls just don't tell boys what they're thinking about, because most boys are afraid of intelligence. We have to pretend we're stupid."

Dara sat up. "Have you done that?"

She was quiet a moment before answering. "No. But I think that's one of the reasons I've never had a real boyfriend. Oh I have friends who are boys and I can be myself with them, but it's not the same thing."

Dara was surprised. He had been admiring the way the sun shone on her hair and was thinking to himself that her eyes were as blue as the Lough. "I can't believe no one has fancied you!"

Gwen coloured at the compliment and remembered Midir. How quickly her life had changed this summer! "Well, one person has," she admitted happily.

Dara grinned. "I knew it. You're very pretty."

She threw him a look of distrust and was suddenly uncomfortable.

"What's wrong?" he asked.

"Don't you think—" she bit her lip "—I'm over-weight?"

He was surprised again. "You're not skin and bones, if that's what you mean. You're lovely. I couldn't help but notice when your clothes were wet."

Gwen blushed furiously but was nonetheless delighted.

He moved a little closer. "I've never met anyone like you. Intelligent, courageous . . ."

Gwen drew back a little. "Maybe I like you just because you're good-looking." She surprised herself. Was she becoming a flirt? But this was truly the reason she liked him—he was so easy to talk to, she could tease him as well.

He let out a guffaw. "I hope you also respect my mind."

They laughed together and then it happened naturally. Both leaned forward for a long slow kiss.

"Better make that two."

"Two kisses?"

"Two people who fancy you. And, yes, the other as well."

CHAPTER TWENTY-THREE

When they left the fort, the two held hands as they wandered back to the road. Gwen grinned to herself as she imagined how she looked, walking casually with a "boyfriend."

"I could run up a mountain without stopping for breath," she said.

Dara squeezed her hand to show he knew what she meant and that he felt the same way. "Will we climb the Cairn? There's a path near here."

Inch Top was the highest point on the island. Sheep grazed in the lower pastures, but the trail grew steeper and stonier the further up they went. Below them fell the island like a multi-coloured map: checkered fields, rocky beaches and pale sandy shores. The wide blue Lough of Swilly glimmered in the sunlight.

"It's called the Lake of Shadows," Dara said, "but it's really 'the lake of eyes.' Swilly is *Súiligh* in Irish, and *súil* means eye. A monster called Súileach, 'full of eyes,' once dwelled in it."

"You know so much about this place. You really love it, don't you?"

"It can be very isolated in the winter. Wild winds and storms. Sometimes the causeway is washed out and we're an island again. I spend every Christmas here."

"What? I thought you lived here!"

"Not at all. My parents moved to Galway when I was little. I stay with Granny every summer to do odd jobs for her, and we all come up for Christmas. She's not really my grandmother, by the way, she's my great-aunt. Everyone calls her Granny instead of Grania."

"But I thought, I mean, you being king and all. You seem to belong here. Like the mountain itself." She blushed, realizing she was painting a romantic picture.

Aware of that, Dara grinned. "You're so North American, Gwen. Everything's either/or. Of course I belong here. This is where my family comes from, generation after generation. These are my 'roots,' as you would say. But I couldn't make a living here any more than my parents could. I'm not a farmer or a fisherman. We own a drapery shop. I'll go into business myself when I leave college. I'll always come back to Inch and I'll probably retire here someday, but my life is elsewhere."

"What does Granny think of you being a businessman?" Gwen was trying to keep her dismay in check.

"She thinks it's brilliant. I'll have a chance at a job, which is something akin to the Holy Grail these days. I'd love to be hired by a big European company. Things will really pick up when our economy is more closely linked to—"

Dara's excitement over a United Europe died when he caught Gwen's look. He stopped to cup her face in his hands. "What on earth is wrong?"

With anyone else she might have hidden it, but with him she didn't want to lie or pretend. "It all sounds so ordinary."

A flash of impatience crossed his features, then he relented. "Ach, Gwen! Do you think Ireland is a garden of dreams? It's a real place with real people in it, and we have to make our living like everyone else in the world."

"But what about Fairyland?" she persisted, "and the things Granny knows and your ancient kingship?"

Dara started to laugh. "You're being either/or again. I don't put everything into separate boxes. I live with all of it."

Suddenly Gwen understood, not only him but herself as well. That was what had been missing in her dealings with the fairies. Either. Or. Practical reality. Airy Fairyland. *She* was the one who made them opposites and then kept changing her mind about which was best. And here were Granny and Dara, comfortable with both, because they did not see the worlds as mutually exclusive.

The two continued up the mountain arm in arm, talking about their lives, their families, their plans for the future. As the path got steeper they were forced to break apart, needing both hands to pull themselves over the rock face. Dara went ahead to scout the way, turning back now and then to call out encouragement.

At one point, Gwen looked behind her to admire the blue waters of the Lough. Something caught her eye. Was she imagining it? She narrowed her gaze against the glare.

There was a shadow on the lake's surface. A dark streak, like a snake. It was very large to be visible at this distance. An undertow perhaps? But it was moving toward the shore. The shadow of a cloud? She glanced up at the sky. It was almost clear. Dara was too far ahead to draw his attention to it. Gwen hurried to catch up, but then stopped to look back again. Her heart jumped.

The shadow had moved onto the shore and was flowing over the sand like a slick of oil. As it inched its way toward the road, she began to panic. She called out to Dara, but the wind buffed her words. Now the shadow slid onto the mountain, up the trail they had taken. Mesmerized, like a small bird waiting for a cobra to pounce, Gwen was unable to move or cry out.

Dara had finally conquered the slippery patch that needed all his attention and turned back to check on Gwen. It took only a second for the image to enter his mind: Gwen's small figure, her back toward him, and the slithering shadow only feet away. As always when faced with the other world, he acted on impulse and intuition. Even he was not aware of the change that came over him, though he raced recklessly down the cliff so cautiously climbed just before. For it was not a boy in blue jeans who was running to Gwen's rescue, but a taller figure who strode with royal confidence and command. The faint echo of a mantle trailed behind him.

When he reached Gwen, he stepped in front of her and held up his hand. "You cannot pass!" he cried imperiously. "Be gone, foul creature, from the presence of the king!"

A shudder passed through the dark shape even as Gwen shuddered behind Dara. Then it was gone and she was free. She put her hand to her eyes as Dara turned to hold her.

"Are you all right?"

"Was that the fairies?" She shook with revulsion.

"The fairies can be spiteful," Dara said, "but they are never evil. That was something else. It's what I was afraid of, what I hoped wouldn't happen. We must get away from here!"

"What are you talking about?"

"Not here," he urged, catching her hand. "That was only the shadow. If the real thing . . ."

He didn't have to say more. Gwen was not only keeping up with him, she was leading the way, pulling his arm to make him run faster. That thing had come for *her*, and she wasn't waiting around for other versions of its horror.

When they reached the road, they continued running till they burst through Granny's door together.

"The shadow of the Hunter," Dara gasped between breaths. "It came out of the lake!"

Granny was already nodding before he finished, and he saw the remains of her oracle on the kitchen table. A moonstone surrounded by a ring of candles and a lunar chart marked with calculations and dates.

"It's the seventh year," she said with dread in her voice. "The time of the Hunter's Moon."

CHAPTER TWENTY-FOUR

GWEN WAS SHIVERING THOUGH it wasn't cold. Granny sat her by the hearth as Dara lit a fire. Though their simple actions comforted her, Gwen knew they were preparing to tell her bad news. It was Granny who explained.

"Fairyland is a wondrous dream in many ways, but every world casts a shadow and even in paradise there was a serpent. Beyond the gates of Faërie lies an all-consuming chaos in the shape of a Great Worm. Crom Cruac is his name and he is also called the Hunter. Driven from Fairyland at the dawn of time, immortal and indestructible, he is kept at bay by a form of tribute.

"Every seven years by the fairy calendar, which can be centuries or more in human terms, a hostage is yielded up to his devouring appetite. If this were not so, he would rise up and devour Fairyland itself. Even as the Great Worm exacts a tribute from the fairies, they in turn exact a tribute from us. The sacrifice, the hostage, is taken from our race.

"While most mortals enter Fairyland at different times unharmed, whoever has the misfortune to arrive in the seventh year becomes the hostage purely by fate. I think you know what this means, my dear Gwen, though it pains me to be the one to tell you."

"Findabhair," Gwen whispered. She felt numb. "Is that why he came for me? Because we're cousins?"

Granny reached out to clasp Gwen's hand. "You are linked to her by name and kinship, but also by fairy law itself. When Finvarra came for her at Tara, you were included in the claim, though he did not succeed. Had he taken two hostages, his gain would have been double-fold. One to live as his bride, the other to die as his sacrifice."

"Tricky divil indeed," Gwen muttered bitterly.

She had recovered enough to consider the facts. For a moment her heart sank as she almost accepted defeat. Then something inside her flared up like the fire.

"My battle with the King continues. I don't accept this. And I don't care if it's tradition or law or what. Findabhair does not deserve to die and even if she did, I would still fight against it. I'm going to find her and help her escape."

Granny raised her eyebrows. Dara let out a whoop. "I'm with you girl! Come hell or high water!"

"Very aptly put" was Granny's warning. "You

mean to defy the fairies, but it may well bring the Hunter down upon us."

"I have to do it," Gwen insisted. "I can't abandon her."

"Come on, Gran," Dara urged. "You know you're with us. Life's a risk and you've always taken it."

Granny managed a smile, though she was obviously troubled. "You're right of course. I wouldn't let you go alone. We will challenge the fairies for Findabhair's life. But there's more at stake than I originally feared. If we fail, we could lose Gwen as well."

"I'm willing to take the chance," Gwen stated.

"We have your arts, Granny," Dara pointed out. "And my hereditary powers by right of kingship. It's a gamble but some of the odds are with us."

"Then we confront the fairies tonight," declared Granny. "For better or worse, the battle is joined."

At twilight the three set out on the path to Dunfinn. Brambles and wild raspberry blocked their way, but Granny went in front with her blackthorn stick to part the sea of greenery. Waves of bracken and fern rose up to their shoulders. The soft muddy ground sucked at their boots. It was as if Nature herself was warning them to turn back.

They came to a spinney of hawthorn trees that grew on a promontory overlooking a marsh. It was a forlorn and desolate place, unlike the other parts of the island Gwen had seen. An eerie silence hung over the meadow grass. The bullrushes stood at attention, a guard of pale spears.

"This marsh is Dunfinn," Granny explained. "The fairy palace is beneath it, deep underground. Mortal feet sink when they tread upon it. We'll stay here till they come to meet us."

The three stood at the edge of the spinney, keeping watch over Dunfinn. All eyes and ears, they awaited some sign that would herald the approach of the fairy folk: a blast of wind, a rising mist, or the echo of music high up in the air. But though the night deepened and clouds sailed over the moon, the silence and emptiness remained unbroken. More than an hour later they were still alone with only the shadows of the trees for company.

"Why do they not come?" Granny muttered. "They know we are here. Are they being devious?"

Her uncertainty affected the younger two. They were feeling small and vulnerable, hemmed in by the darkness.

The crackle of twigs behind them caught all by surprise.

"Findabhair!" Gwen cried.

For there stood her cousin, looking perfectly normal, in her own clothes and with her knapsack perched on her back. A quick glance round the spinney confirmed she was alone.

Gwen ran to embrace her. "Your life is in danger!

Not just from the fairies. We've got to get you away!"

"If you mean the Hunter's Moon, cuz, I already know." Findabhair's voice was strangely calm. "Finvarra told me himself. He's madly in love with me and doesn't want me to be the sacrifice."

"So he set you free!" Gwen cried with delight.

Once again the Fairy King had turned the tables, but in this case Gwen didn't mind at all. Bubbling over with happiness, she introduced Dara and Granny, describing breathlessly to Findabhair their intentions to save her.

"You're so American, Gwen," Findabhair said quietly. "Did I ever ask to be saved?"

Gwen was brought up short by the remark, and Dara looked puzzled, but Granny's voice was stern. "Tell her the truth, girl, or I will. I see the mark on your brow."

Findabhair looked at Granny as if for the first time and recognized another who had lived among the fairies. Then, with a deep sigh, she put her arm around Gwen.

"I've only come back for a little while. To say my goodbyes. I'm still the hostage, by my own consent."

CHAPTER TWENTY-FIVE

"COME AWAY FROM THIS place," Granny ordered quickly.

Though Gwen allowed herself to be hustled from Dunfinn and back to Granny's without a word, her mind raced with what Findabhair had said. When they were safely inside the cottage, she let loose.

"Are you crazy? This is the absolute limit. You're too young to die and it isn't even your battle. I've put up with your selfishness all through this adventure, off doing your own thing regardless of how it might affect anyone, but this takes the cake. I can tell you right now, Findabhair Folan, you're not going to do it. Do you hear me? The word is *no!*"

Dara stood in silent support as Gwen raged and wept. Findabhair looked pale and sad. She didn't respond to the attack but hung her head like the guilty party. When Gwen grew quiet, Granny drew them all to the fire.

"Why have you chosen to do this, dear one?" she asked.

Findabhair slumped in her seat and gazed at the flames. "For the sake of Fairyland." Her voice was low, almost inaudible. "If I don't do it, they'll all be destroyed and the land of Faërie itself. Like the other hostages before me, I go willingly. No mortal has ever been forced.

"I'm not going alone. Finvarra goes with me. He will abdicate his throne and let Midir rule instead. We had a terrible row over it. He was going to take my place but I wouldn't allow it, and that is my right as the sacrifice. He would do it out of love for me and his kingdom. I do it for the same reason.

"Don't you see?" she pleaded with her cousin. "It *is* my battle. I am the Queen of Fairyland."

Gwen clenched her fists. No matter how much she hated it, she did understand the decision. The rescue of Fairyland. It was in all the old tales. Many a human had risked everything to keep that wondrous land alive. But how could she choose between Faërie and Findabhair? The death of either was impossible to accept. She sat up suddenly.

"If the hostages have always gone willingly, doesn't that mean there has never been a fight? Could we challenge Crom Cruac? Save both Findabhair and Fairyland?"

Dara let out a low whistle. "By my kingship, we'll try!"

Both were stunned into silence by the immensity of what they proposed.

Granny too appeared awed, but she nodded slowly. "All things are possible between heaven and earth. I had a feeling we were heading for something momentous."

The gist of their talk finally dawned on Findabhair.

"You mean you're willing to go with me and Finvarra? And not only that, but to fight?" A flush of excitement brought colour to her cheeks. For the first time that night she looked her old self. "We need a battle plan!"

"Welcome back, cuz." Gwen grinned. "I missed you."

They all began talking at once, but Granny took command. "We need a strategy," she agreed, "but if the King has chosen to face Crom Cruac, he should be here also."

"Would he know . . . " Gwen began.

"He'll know," said Granny and Findabhair.

For a moment the old woman and young girl regarded each other.

"Will it be difficult for you?" Findabhair asked.

"No, but what about you?"

"I've never been the jealous sort," was the frank reply. "That's why I get along with them so well."

Only after Finvarra arrived did the others understand the meaning of this exchange.

When the King of Faërie entered the little kitchen, it was as if a panther had stalked into the room. In that cosy, very human setting, he appeared all the more wild and preternatural. Cloaked in black night, glittering with stars, he barely contained his boundless power. As he stepped through the door a gust of wind followed, blowing leaves over the threshold.

Instinctively the four humans bowed toward the King. To their surprise, he bowed back.

"Greetings, companions. I come to you most happily. Your decision this night resounds through the halls of Faërie like a call to arms."

He spoke to each in turn. On Dara's shoulder he laid his hand. "Hail, King of Inch. I have known your ancestors, your line is noble. I am glad that you join me on this perilous venture."

"All kings and princes look to the High King," Dara replied formally. "It is my honour to stand by you, sire."

Gwen was beside Dara, and Finvarra addressed her next. There was a smile on his lips, but his look was one of admiration and respect. "My buttercup has become a mountain rose. A warrior maiden of high courage and strength. It was a game well-played, and you won against the odds. It is good, methinks, to have the victor on *my* side."

Gwen was shy. She still found him overwhelming. "I'm glad we're no longer enemies," she said, and she meant it.

"Then we shall be friends," he replied.

When he came to Granny, he took her hand and bowed over it as he placed it to his lips. There was a wistfulness to his actions, which had become extremely gentle. "Dear heart. Thou art not forgotten. Always my people have watched over you and blessed you."

"I know that," Granny said. "And it has meant much to me."

"You never married? I would not have wished that for you."

"It was my decision," she said firmly. Then a girlish laugh lit up her features. "There was no one who could replace you."

In that moment the others caught a glimpse of an old truth. Granny suddenly appeared as she was in her youth, Grania Harte, a dark-haired beauty who had once been consort to the King of the Fairies. Then the image faded and there she stood, grey-haired and aged, but still tall and unbowed.

Lastly, Finvarra came to Findabhair. He didn't touch her and yet his very stance was a caress, inclining toward her like a reed in the wind. "We need no words, Beloved. Our fates are entwined. It is for you I have taken this path and I do so without regret. Whether fairy or mortal, love is all."

Her empathy with his speech was evident in the light that transformed her. Findabhair was no longer a girl but a woman, in the presence of the one she loved and with whom she would willingly die.

Finvarra had been acting in the manner of a High King, with the genteel *courteisie* of the fairy race. Now he dropped his stately pose to stand before them in modern dress, a young man with dark eyes that were sad and solemn.

"We go as equals, friends, to confront our doom. For no one yet has survived the Hunter's Moon."

ChAPTER TWENTY-SIX

It was late into the night and the hearth flickered fitfully as the last flames collapsed into embers. Shadows danced on the walls. Voices rose and fell in earnest murmurs. The little group hunched over the mountain of books that was Granny's library of ancient wisdom. Some were thin volumes, others heavy tomes, with faded lettering, hieroglyphics and indecipherable words. Some were illustrated with fabulous designs, while others were plain with a secret power of their own.

"Every magician's treasure trove," Granny explained, as she produced yet another pile from under the stairs, "is their store of charms and spells and prophetic utterances. Somewhere in these pages we will find what we need."

Gwen threw Findabhair a despairing look. Despite hours of searching they had yet to find anything.

"You must know more about this than any human," Findabhair whispered to Finvarra. Then she looked shamefaced when she realized the others had overheard.

"I know only what has always been known, my love," the King answered gently. "At the heart of the story about your race and mine is this simple truth. Mortals must choose again and again to save Fairyland. If they do not, we die."

"Bigod, here it is!" Dara suddenly cried out. "*A charm against the Great Worm!*"

Granny's hands shook with excitement as she took hold of the book and read out loud. "*To kill a worm wherein there is terror, seven angels from paradise may do so valiantly.*"

When no one else commented, Gwen finally asked, "So what does that mean?"

"Our endeavour is possible," said Finvarra thoughtfully.

"If we find seven angels," Findabhair snorted.

"We've got five right here," was Dara's suggestion. "We'll do it short-handed."

"No!" Granny's slate-grey eyes were as hard as iron. She gripped the book of spells in her left hand like a sword. "Fools rush in where angels fear to tread. If we are to challenge the universe, we'll follow the ancient guides. To do otherwise would be arrogance, the seal of our doom. Either we find two more or give up this quest."

Exhausted from trying to grasp on to hope, Findabhair spoke bitterly. "Two more who believe in fairies in this day and age? And not only that, who love them enough to risk their own lives? We've as much chance as—"

Gwen slapped the arm of her chair with a report like gunshot. "There are two more! Right here in Ireland! Two friends of mine! Wow, I can hardly believe this. It's as if—" She stopped. Her eyes shone with wonder. "This is all meant to happen." She shrugged and grinned shyly as the others stared at her, amazed. "Well, I can't be one hundred per cent sure until I ask them, but I'm pretty certain we've two more."

The deep furrow that marked Granny's brow disappeared. Her words rang with a new confidence that inspired them all. "Seven were the days of Genesis. Seven are the pillars of life. Seven will be the fires of the Apocalypse. No better number can ride the storm. As a Company of Seven we will forge our destiny."

Gwen's promise to summon her friends ended the night's deliberations. The fire had smouldered into ash. The room was cold. Finvarra glanced at the window restlessly.

"I can bide here no longer," he said, standing to bow. "Till we meet again, companions."

Findabhair left with him to walk in the garden. The scent of flowers perfumed the night air. Moonlight dappled fields and hedgerows, making a silver vein of the road that circled the island.

"Mortal dwellings are too close for me," the King explained softly.

He was already assuming fairy shape, blending into the shadows of the landscape, rising into the dark sky studded with stars.

"Go freely, my love," Findabhair whispered, "till we meet again."

When he stooped to kiss her, it was as if the wind caressed her lips, a warm wind but wild too, tasting of earth and leaves and rain-moist air.

As she returned to the house, Gwen met her in the doorway.

"It's impossible," Findabhair said, tears trickling down her face.

Gwen gave her a hug. "Nothing's impossible, cuz. After all we've been through, you should know that by now."

Dara had made up the sofa bed in the kitchen for himself, leaving his room for the two girls. They were still talking when dawn arrived, not only of the adventure that lay ahead but of the ones each had had when they were apart.

"I'm really sorry, Gwen," Findabhair said, when she heard her cousin's story. "I wasn't much help, was I? I got so caught up with Finvarra I hadn't a thought in my head for anything else. I used to hate girls who dropped their pals because of a fellow. But now I know how being madly in love can do that to you. You must have been so angry with me."

"Funny about that," Gwen said. "I was and I wasn't. I mean, once I got the hang of it, I was actually glad I was on my own, doing everything for myself and making all the decisions. If you had been there, I would have been following you around like a dope as I always did. And another thing," she added, in a moment of total honesty, "I was really glad you weren't here when I met Dara."

"Oh God, yes, what a sweetie. We would have been tearing out each other's hair for him."

They muffled their laughter under the blankets.

"Is he your boyfriend?"

"Yes. Keep your eyes and your hands off him."

More giggles. Then Findabhair sighed with envy. "You're the lucky one. At least he's in the same world as you."

"Huh. Canada and Ireland are as far apart as Ireland and Faërie. We're both in for long-distance relationships."

They sighed together.

"And who knows if we'll even have that by the time this is over," Gwen said in a low voice.

Findabhair shuddered. "Call me Scarlett, but I'm not going to think about that till tomorrow."

Though Findabhair eventually fell asleep, Gwen stayed awake, staring up at the ceiling. Oddly enough, she felt excited instead of tired, as if she were expecting something wonderful to happen. At the first tap on her window, she knew. They were out there waiting for her.

Dressed in the long T-shirt she wore to bed, Gwen crept silently from the room and out of the cottage. The early morning was soft and misty and all a pale glow. The dewy grass was cool beneath her bare feet. A breeze stroked her face like a gentle caress. When at last she spied them, the laughter bubbled on her lips. Her childhood dream come true. Fairies at the end of the garden!

It was just as she had always imagined. Sitting on the tip of every leaf, they covered the hedgerow like a mass of bright berries. Tiny and winged, clothed in thistledown and spider web, golden-haired, silver-eyed, shining like fireflies. Their size took nothing from the wonder of their creation. Does the speck of a star diminish its beauty? Indeed Gwen gazed upon this cluster of fairies with the same awe she viewed the constellations of heaven. Here was infinite life in all its splendour.

"Thank you," she whispered, with tears in her eyes.

She knew who had sent this precious gift. After all the hardship he had caused her, Gwen was now fully reconciled with the King of Faërie.

CHAPTER TWENTY-SEVEN

KATIE QUIRKE STRAPPED THE luggage onto her motorbike, while her mother and sisters waited nearby to say their farewells. All were unanimously agreed that she deserved this holiday and kept offering their assurances that they could run the farm without her. One last time Katie clung to her mother, whose own tears were beginning to fall.

"Enough of this nonsense, girl," Mrs. Quirke said gruffly. "You're well overdue a break. You just forget about us and enjoy yourself, do you hear?"

Katie nodded obediently and made an effort to control herself, but she couldn't help wondering if she would ever see her family again. From Gwen's phone call, she knew the nature of the mission she faced, knew that it was dangerous and its outcome uncertain. And yet, though it made this parting painful, wild horses couldn't have kept her away.

Katie pulled on her yellow mack like a cloak and eased her helmet over her head. As if girded for battle, she mounted the bike and waved her last goodbyes. Then down the Burren road she sped, on the first lap of her journey into the north.

Driving through the town of Kilcolgan, she was overtaken by a silver Mercedes. The sunshine struck its roof with a burst of light, and instinctively Katie raised her arm to salute the driver. More than an hour later, as she left Claremorris, the same car passed her again with a friendly beep. She had already decided to stop for lunch in Sligo when she spotted the Mercedes parked in front of a hotel. On an impulse, she drew up her bike and, with her helmet under her arm, went in search of its owner.

The hotel was softly lit and plushy, with a narrow hallway leading to a lounge bar and dining room. Katie scanned the crowd in the bar. Though she had no idea what the driver looked like, she hoped he would recognize her mack and helmet. When a stocky red-haired man in a business suit stood up to signal, Katie hurried to his table. She was only faintly surprised to see the platter of sandwiches with more than enough for two.

"This is a wild but educated guess," she said. "Are you Mattie O'Shea?"

"Katie Quirke, I presume?" He put out his hand.

The two redheads grinned at each other with instant liking.

"I hoped you'd see the car and ordered some lunch for you," he explained, as Katie pulled off her mack and sat down. "Will you take a drink?"

"Pint of Guinness. This is grand. I'm starving."

When Mattie came back with two pints of stout, they lifted their glasses in a toast.

"To the high road."

"And beyond."

"Gwen said you offered me a lift in your car, but I prefer to travel alone. And I wanted time to think. You didn't mind?"

"Not at all," said Mattie. "It worked out for the best. I had a few matters to clear up just in case . . . Do you know, when I passed you near Galway, I knew it was you. For a moment I saw something else. Not a girl on a motorbike, but a giantess on a horse!"

His face flushed, as redheads' are wont to do, and he was about to apologize for talking nonsense, but Katie reassured him.

"When the sunlight hit your Mercedes, it looked like a silver chariot. That's why I waved. Strange doings are afoot and we are already part of them."

They stared at each other in silence, aware of the huge nameless thing they were moving toward.

"You have a wife and family? Was it hard for you to leave them?"

Mattie sighed heavily. "It was. But I had a long talk with Miriam, and she agrees with what I'm doing. We both come from villages where the old ways haven't died out altogether. It seems right to go when you are called. What about you?"

"I lied," Katie said guiltily. "Officially I'm on holidays. They have enough on their plates with my Da ill and the farm to look after. I don't want to add to their worries. I'm worried myself about what might happen, but that couldn't or wouldn't stop me. I feel as if my whole life has been a preparation for this. I even finally managed to quit smoking, to purify myself in a way. Does that sound daft?"

"Not to me," said Mattie. His middle-aged features were suddenly youthful as the imaginative boy inside him crowed with approval.

When they left the hotel, the two parted as friends.

"Safe journey till we meet again on Inch!"

★   ★   ★

When the sleek silver car pulled up outside Granny's cottage, Gwen ran to greet Mattie. The others were a little surprised by his professional appearance, but it wasn't long before he was ensconced in the kitchen.

It was a good while later, when they were finishing supper, that Katie arrived. Her motorcycle belched a cloud of black smoke as it came to a halt with a splutter. Again Gwen ran out to meet her friend, though this reunion was louder as they hugged with shouts of glee.

"I was in a fit I wouldn't make it," Katie cried.

"Bloody potholes! The exhaust is broken and maybe more. But even if the blasted thing fell apart, I would have come by foot if I had to."

Helmet under her arm, she marched into the house and greeted Mattie like a long-lost brother. Then she shook hands with the others, pumping their arms with a good grip. All were impressed by her boundless energy.

"Are you hungry, my dear?" Granny asked. "I've kept your dinner in the oven."

"God bless you."

The others ate their dessert as Katie started in on her bacon and cabbage. With many bursts of hilarity, the talk around the table was uninhibited. It was as if there were no strangers present. And as the personalities blended and grew more familiar, each was overcome by the feeling they had met before. In another time, another place, this group had gathered. Was it simply their destiny to do so again?

"Are we all here?" Mattie asked, looking around. "I have the sense that someone is missing. As if I'm holding a meeting and my top salesman is absent."

"You too?" Katie exclaimed. "I was thinking myself the count was wrong." She started to laugh, "A head short of the herd."

Pleased that the circle was melding so well, Granny gave Gwen a look that implied the time had come.

Gwen cleared her throat. "There was something I left out in the phone calls. As you've guessed yourselves, there is another with us. I thought it might be a bit too much to give you the whole story all in one go."

Katie caught her breath as a shiver of premonition ran through her. She knew Gwen was about to say something wonderful.

"The King of the Fairies is in this with us."

Katie released her breath in a whistle. Mattie went pale.

"That's it!" cried Katie. "Now I'll die happy."

"Let's hope we won't have to," Findabhair warned.

Mattie held himself stiffly to contain his excitement. His boyhood wish was about to be fulfilled. "When will he join us?"

"He has asked us to meet him tonight at Inch Castle," said Gwen.

"It's an empty ruin," Dara explained, "but he's uncomfortable in houses."

"A midnight court?" Katie asked overjoyed.

"A Council of War" was the sobering reply.

CHAPTER TWENTY-EIGHT

SOMETIME BEFORE MIDNIGHT, they set out for Inch Castle in Mattie's car. Granny sat in the front seat while the four young people went in the back.

"You'll have to sit on my lap," Dara said, pulling Gwen down as she got into the car.

"There's plenty of room," she protested mildly.

"No there isn't." He held her firmly and nuzzled the back of her neck.

Findabhair rolled her eyes at Katie, who grinned.

"Everyone comfortable back there?" asked Mattie.

"Some of us more than others," was Findabhair's reply.

They drove to the far side of the island where a silver cattle gate led into the field that bordered Inch Castle. Cropped short by sheep, the grass was like a manicured lawn, glowing dimly in the starlight. With a gentle lilt, the land rolled downwards to where a rocky lakeshore met the dark waters of the Lough. A mist snaked like a scarf along the shore. Standing starkly against the horizon was a broken tooth of stone: the ruins of Inch Castle overgrown with ivy.

As the little group made their way toward it, Dara told the most notorious tale of the castle's history.

"Two cousins were fighting for the kingship of Donegal, and one locked the other inside the tower. When the castle was set ablaze, the prisoner broke free and came out on the battlements. His cousin was below, camped in this very field. Donnell—on the ramparts—dislodged a huge rock and hurled it down on Rury's head. Needless to say, Donnell became king."

"God, what a story," said Katie. "Those ancient lads were pure wild."

As Dara finished his tale, the air around Inch Castle began to waver. All of them saw the scene. Flames lit up the night sky with a red glow. Men crowded below the walls, weapons glinting. A figure stood on the ramparts, maddened and roaring. As he lifted a great stone . . .

"Look away," said Granny quickly. "Stop thinking about it. Time and space are awry near the fairy folk."

Even as they obeyed her, the din of war receded and the ghosts of the past disappeared. The castle did not return to ruins, however, but stood now as it had in its heyday.

Finely pointed and mortared, the tower rose

grandly, blocks of grey stone interlaced with white granite. Present also were the wings and buttresses that had long since fallen into the sea. Tasselled banners fluttered from the turrets. The citadel was ablaze with light. Chandeliers could be seen through the vaulted windows. Music issued forth over fields and lake. The group quickened their pace, knowing what this meant. Fairy revels were taking place within.

As the six approached the great oaken door of the castle, it swung open of its own accord. Gay sounds rushed out to greet them: unrestrained chatter and laughter, music incredibly wild and merry. When all had crossed over the threshold, the fairy tale began anew.

They found themselves clothed in rich raiment and bedecked with jewels. Katie was resplendent in yellow silk with her shoulders bare and her hair caught up in combs of gold. Granny was a stately matron in silver-grey with a train of ermine draped behind her. Gwen twirled with delight in her rose-coloured gown embroidered all over with wild red roses. Findabhair's beauty was accented once again in her favourite black, a sheen of sleek satin stippled with pearls. The men were no less bright in hose and doublets, with capes tossed back dashingly over one shoulder. Dara was in scarlet like the famous Pimpernel, Mattie in brown velvet with a jaunty plumed hat.

Everything was arranged for fun and frolic. Tables groaned beneath the weight of a fabulous feast, sweet-meats and savouries and every possible confection.

Marble fountains dispensed the liquid: red wines flowing warmly, white wines running cool and champagne bubbling like a mountain stream. The hall reverberated with tumultuous tunes as the assembly capered on deft feet without stopping for breath.

"Council of War?" Gwen said, laughing.

"The fairy way." Findabhair grinned. "We should have known. Party first, get serious later."

"Proper order," Katie declared as she looked around her with satisfaction. "At least I'll get a taste of what I'm fighting for."

But there was no more time to talk. The fairy folk came running to fetch them to the ball.

Dara eventually managed to catch up with Gwen, who had been drawn away by Midir. Though the red-haired captain yielded his partner, it was not without reluctance.

"I think he fancies you," Dara said.

"As a matter of fact, he does," Gwen replied airily.

A furrow of jealousy creased Dara's brow.

Gwen started to laugh. "Men are so ridiculous. Always forgetting the important question. Who do *I* like?"

Dara laughed too as he caught her in his arms. "Don't you mean, who do you *love*?"

"Maybe," she said. Yes, she had definitely become a flirt.

"Let's get stuck into the feast," Dara suggested, heading for the banquet tables.

Gwen let go of his hand. "Don't you remember what I told you?" she said wincing. "How I failed the trial?"

"You and a hundred thousand others. According to Granny, who failed it too, you'd have to *hate* food to pass the test."

"That certainly wouldn't be me," Gwen said ruefully. Then she brightened as the truth struck home. "And you know what? I like being me. To hell with diets. Where's that chocolate mousse?"

It was sometime later when Midir discovered Katie, and the two redheads danced onto the floor with wild abandon.

"This is the life!" Katie cried, as the hall spun round.

"It could be yours, if you wish."

"Go 'way with you. You're sweeping me off my feet."

Mattie wouldn't dance at first, despite the entreaties of the beautiful fairy women. He stood at the edge of the crowd, gazing in quiet bliss like one enchanted. The fairies whispered amongst themselves.

"Will our guest not dance?"

"He will, he will. She's on her way."

"Has the King sent for her?"

"Of course. You'll see."

Though Mattie overheard them, he didn't understand until he saw her. Dressed in a blue gown with a girdle of sapphires, she moved through the crowd as gracefully as a swan.

"Miriam! What on earth—" He ran to embrace her but stopped, suddenly awed as he had been when they first courted. Instead, he took off his plumed hat and bowed before her.

"Matt, is this a dream? Or are we really together in Fairyland?"

"I think the answer is yes to both, my love. Shall we dance?"

Granny too was drawn onto the floor, for in Faërie no limbs are old or weary. Fond cries surrounded her—"Grania, you have returned to us!"—as the fairies greeted a former Queen.

It was the same for Findabhair, their present Queen. Wherever she walked, they gathered around her, kissing her hand and murmuring their affection. Though she was touched by their attentions and agreed to dance, her eyes kept searching the hall. She was well used to fairy custom and knew that Finvarra would be late, but she couldn't enjoy herself until he arrived. Wandering away from the crowd, she stood alone in an alcove overlooking Lough Swilly.

The moon was mirrored in the water, rippling with waves. It was as if a pale-gold creature, precious and fragile, swam just beneath the surface. In the distance, the dark mountains kept watch like sentinels.

"I wish this would stop," she sighed to herself.

But then again, no. It was something she had never

experienced before. She felt like a moth drawn to the flame, fluttering her wings in vain, unable to break free. Unable even to want to be free.

"It is no easier for me, Beloved," he murmured behind her.

Finvarra's arms encircled her as he laid his head upon her shoulder. Findabhair turned to embrace him.

The King's sloe-black eyes brooded on her. "I have always loved freely, never losing myself utterly in any one woman. You have disrupted my life as greatly as I have yours."

"Is that supposed to make me feel better?" she said, when in fact it did.

He saw this and his humour lightened. "It was your name that first drew me to you, my sweet Findabhair. So like to mine and none other bears it. I should have been warned instead of drawn. It is doom to meet one's equal."

Findabhair laughed as the King grasped her tighter to show how meaningless were his words. "I missed you," she said.

"Only three days, *a stór*, and did I not come to you each night?"

"That was really you? I thought it was only my dreams."

"Dreams are never 'only,' " he chided. "But come, my Queen, it is not love but war that we must look to this night."

They stepped out from the alcove, one human,

one immortal, both clothed in night's black and arrayed with stars. As they walked arm in arm toward the assembly, the music and dancing ceased and trumpets blared.

"Make way for the King and Queen of Faërie!"

CHAPTER TWENTY-NINE

FROM THEIR VARIOUS CORNERS
of the hall, the others came to meet the King. Finvarra greeted them warmly, especially the newcomers
whom Gwen presented.

"Dearest Caitlín," he said to Katie, kissing her
hand. "The finest woman that ever went into the walls
of a farm." He used a Burren expression to honour
her, and she coloured with pleasure. "Have we mended
your walls well? Have we kept guard over your herds?"

"Your people have always been good to me, sir."

"And you have always been a good neighbour to us."

He touched a stray tress of her dark-red hair and
tucked it back into place. "You put me in mind of my
Tánaiste. Perhaps one day, my sweet, you will tire of
mortal toil and join him in Fairyland."

Katie's eyebrows shot up like two birds leaving the
branch.

"Something to think about when the going gets rough," the King whispered in her ear.

"Hail to you, Maitiú," he said, turning to Mattie who was holding his wife's hand. "Your family are known to me from past generations. Your great-grandfather stood before me even as you do now."

Mattie's eyes widened. "So that old tale was true! My granny always maintained he had drink taken that night."

The King of the Fairies burst into laughter. "You have kept faith with us, despite modern disbelief. A brave stance for a man of business."

Mattie squared his shoulders. "Some old beliefs hold up progress, but there's no point in throwing out the baby with the bath water. Why go blindly into the future with nothing at our backs?"

"Spoken like a champion!" Finvarra declared.

"And good evening to you, *mo chara*," he said to Miriam, who curtsied before him. "Have you enjoyed my feast?"

"Very much, sir, thank you," she said. Then her smile wavered. "But I think I know why you invited me."

He nodded sadly. "It was not an easy thing you did when you gave your husband leave to answer our call. We are most grateful to you. I will do my best to ensure this is not a final parting."

Miriam turned to Mattie to hold him tightly, then she stiffened suddenly. "The baby's crying. I must go.

You are in good company, my dearest. I can only pray that they will bring you back to me."

Mattie kissed his wife before she faded away, returning to her bed where she was waking at the sound of a child's cry.

"Now friends, it is time we held our council," the King announced. "A room has been prepared."

They followed him up a winding stone stairway into a large chamber at the top of the castle. Tapestries depicting ancient battles hung on the walls. The fireplace burned whole logs. Vaulted windows looked out on the ramparts and the shadowy mountains. In the centre of the room, flanked by high-backed chairs, was a carved table as round as the moon.

"Like King Arthur's!" Gwen cried, delighted.

"As with his court, we are a company of equals," said Finvarra.

When each was seated, a solemn air fell over all.

Granny rose to open the discussion. "This is a Council of War. We are all agreed that we will defy Crom Cruac. What remains to be decided is how and when. We'll begin with the how of it. Finvarra?"

"There are two gates to Fairyland," the King explained, "which mark the borders of our territory in time though not in space. The White Gates of Morning are the entrance to Faërie. The Black Gates of Night are the exit. It is in the chasm beyond the gates of night that Crom Cruac lies. The hostage is led to the gates on the night of the Hunter's Moon. Once they go beyond, we do not know what befalls them."

Findabhair shuddered, then took comfort from looking around at her friends.

"Crom Cruac is called 'the Great Worm.' Do we know anything more about him?" asked Katie. She wanted to know the worst, to be ready for it.

Once again, Finvarra answered. "I cannot recall a time when he did not exist, but in the early days of the world my people were young and unknowing. Our memories of that time are as dim as your own childhoods. I do know, however, that it was not Faërie that expelled Crom Cruac beyond our gates, though this is said in mortal tales. According to our legends, he was chained there by the archangels after a great war in the Empyrean, a realm higher than our own."

"Oh God, I hope he isn't who I think he is," Katie muttered. "I haven't been to Mass in ages."

Mattie was thinking along the same lines. Only now was he considering the true nature of the beast. Though he had no intentions of turning back, he couldn't help but ask, "Do we dare?"

Granny's look was sympathetic, but her voice was firm. "The mouse may look upon the cobra. The hare upon the hawk. There is no law in the universe that forbids this."

As the company absorbed her words, each accepted the bottom line of what lay ahead.

"You mean we have the right to die trying," Gwen said.

"But we may not die!" Findabhair avowed. "It could be his destiny to die at this time and ours to do the deed."

"Well said, my Queen," Finvarra saluted her.

They sat tall in their chairs, like lords and ladies.

"So be it," Granny concluded. "Together we go beyond the gates, to meet our destiny. The only question left is—when?"

"He rises on the night of the Hunter's Moon," Finvarra said. "That is the ritual. But I also believe it is his time of greatest strength."

"Then we should attack beforehand," Mattie declared. "Catch him off guard and possibly weaker."

"We're already breaking the rules," Katie agreed. "Why keep to the appointed time?"

A ripple of excitement ran round the table as everyone concurred.

"The King of Inch has yet to speak," Finvarra said, regarding Dara curiously.

Dara had been quiet throughout the council, studying the company. He had noted the courage and strength in each voice. Their morale was at its peak after the fairy feast, as with the fêting of warriors in ancient days. He could feel the power in that circle. Newly joined together, they were at their best before minor differences could weaken their unity. He knew that what he was about to propose hadn't occurred to any of them as yet, but for him it was the logical conclusion.

He took a deep breath and stood up. "I say we go tonight. Not later, but this very minute."

As if a thunderclap had struck the room, all jumped to their feet. Of course. The simple truth. There were no preparations to make. If not now, when?

The time of the Hunter's Moon had come.

CHAPTER THIRTY

They stood outside the walls of Inch Castle which had become a dark and empty ruin once more. The night sky was black, with a cold spray of stars. Lake water lapped against the shore. In the distance, a dog barked. The humans in the company drank in this moment, aware that they might never see their world again. The fairy glamour was gone. Their own clothes had returned and with them a sense of vulnerability.

"It's all so sudden," Findabhair murmured. "It changes everything."

"Yeah," sighed Gwen. "My crummy old life doesn't look half bad after all." She glanced at Dara. "And just when things were getting good." She noticed that he was looking shaky, and she moved closer to take his hand.

"I've never felt less like a king," he said. Then he

gave her a long look. "I wish we'd had more time together."

"Me too."

It was one of those moments when everyone felt extremely fond of each other. All were polite and even shy as they exchanged last words and embraces.

"You're the best friend I ever had," Findabhair said to Gwen. "Sorry for being such a bollocks."

"Hang in there, kid. Last one home's a pumpkin."

"Courage, noble hearts," said Granny. "Fairyland will bless us before we face our foe."

Finvarra led them to a mound of grass and stones that stood beside the castle.

"Faërie is everywhere and hence its gates also. But my people favour these tumuli, which have the nature of thresholds. This was a passage grave in days gone by. Even as it once ushered ancient souls on to their journey, so it will take us to the beginning of ours."

They climbed the mound to where a small dolmen was barely visible, overgrown with sods of grass. Finvarra didn't have to stoop as he entered, for he suddenly grew smaller, but the others found it awkward. As they bent low to pass through, each suffered the same moment of discomfort and panic. One by one they were squeezed within the cleft of rock, enclosed by darkness and the smell of damp earth. Then, with a final push like death, like life, they came out on the other side.

"Open one door and you find another," Finvarra

said when they had all come through.

They were in a strange formless place, a milky void. Towering before them was an immense gate of ivory and alabaster and all things white.

"The pearly gates," Gwen said with a grin.

Finvarra smiled back.

"Some mortal once glimpsed it and thought it so, the Gates of Heaven, but it is the White Gates of Morning that bring us to my land."

As the King spoke, the gates swung open and the seven stepped through.

Whether it took seconds or aeons to cross that beautiful country, they couldn't be certain. Time is meaningless in a land suspended between morning and night. It held the breadth of infinity within its borders. And whether the countryside swept past them like wind, or they travelled themselves at impossible speeds, they couldn't be sure either. But it seemed they had taken on hinds' feet as they leaped over mountains and cataracts and the white rush of rivers. Everything shone with a startling light. The glow of an eternal spring day. *For lo, the winter is past, the flowers appear on the earth and the time of the singing of birds is come.*

On the Plain of the Apple Trees they were showered with pink blossoms. In Tír na nÓg they splashed through the fountains of youth. After a deep-sea dive into a warm green ocean, they danced with the mer-people in the Land Below Waves. Over mountains of spices they sailed like birds. The pungent odours wafted skyward like incense from a temple. *Spikenard and saffron, calamus and cinnamon, with all trees of frankincense, myrrh and aloes.*

When they ate of the fruit in an orchard of pomegranates, the fiery seeds burst on their tongues like cool flame. The air resounded with sweet strains of music as if it were a lyre played by invisible hands. The song of forever, the music of the spheres, echoed in every corner of the land. It was a place of melodious harmony and nameless wonders. *A fountain of gardens. A well of living waters.*

Only when they neared the end of their journey were they aware of the change that had occurred. As if they had passed through the waters of rebirth, or the purifying rite of a baptismal fire, each had been transformed. They had taken on the form that was their very soul, no longer inside them, but worn without like a shining garment. Each bore the aspect of what they *might* be.

In a white and gold gown with the signs of the zodiac, Granny reflected the wisdom of the ages. She wore a headdress with two horns that clasped the moon. In her hand was a tall staff with a silver serpent twisting around it. She was the High Priestess.

With the majestic air of ancient sovereignty, Dara had become the archetypal King. In royal purple and a crown of gold, he carried a shield emblazoned with a blood-red dragon. At his side hung the sword Excalibur.

By Dara's right hand stood Mattie, champion of champions. With a shining lance that touched the sky, he wore the tunic and cloak of a Celtic warrior. He held his body erect like a battering ram, and his proud stance spoke of an indomitable will.

The three young women bore the three faces of the Goddess.

Clothed in forest-green, Katie gripped the arc of a great bow in her hands. Over her shoulder was slung a quiver of arrows. Her long red hair was tied back to reveal a cool brow. She was the woman who needed no man, for she was strength herself, the Huntress.

Findabhair was aglow in the colour of sunset, the burning hues of the Goddess of Love. But her aspect was not the gentle one of peaceful times: she exuded passion, the kind that shatters all order to bring empires to their knees. She carried two swords, one in each hand, for love can be double-edged and deadly.

Cloaked in blue, with the calmness of deliberation and judgement, Gwen had a look of stern serenity. In her hand she carried the rapier blade of truth. For she was the upholder of universal law, as impartial and implacable as fate itself.

And how could a Fairy King be transformed? What could be brighter than the ruler of an other-world race? In chain mail of woven light, he carried a golden shield and spear. From his shoulders unfurled two great wings; not the gossamer appendages his own people sported at times, but the swan's span of feathered strength, ribbed with muscle and bone of iron. He had become his higher self, the avenging Archangel.

Arrayed in the blessings of the Land of Ideals, the Company of Seven arrived at their place of destiny. *To kill a worm wherein there is terror, seven angels from paradise may do so valiantly.*

As colossal as the portal that had granted them entrance, the Black Gates of Night loomed before them. With the gleam of ebony and obsidian and all things black, it was like the open maw of boundless space. All were suddenly filled with dread, for they heard the whisper in the darkest recesses of their minds.

Abandon hope, all ye who enter here.

CHAPTER THIRTY-ONE

After journeying through eternal day, they were shocked to arrive in a land of endless night. No light had ever shone here. No sun had risen to warm these shadows. Unable to see in the darkness, they put their own words on the landscape to give it form. The dim shapes in the distance were a range of mountains. They stood on a shore of jagged rock. The black liquid in front of them was a dark tarn, fathomless and still. Cold seeped into their bones with the slow ache of despair. The lack of light and warmth was an agonizing loss.

For the six humans, this was an encounter with the deepest nightmare of their race. It was as if they had been awakened in the dead of night to hear the dread secret uttered. *At the heart of life is a void without purpose or meaning. There is no God. There is no love. All is emptiness and loneliness. Since time began, you have been abandoned.*

Finvarra too was deeply affected. King of a land of light, he viewed night as a time for sport and play. But there was no joy in this darkness, no stars to greet as fellow beings, no creatures to welcome him into their revels. These shadows harboured naught but the Enemy.

Is this the battle? Gwen asked herself. Is the enemy faceless? A thing of the mind?

Following her thoughts, Granny said out loud, "Perhaps the true test is to keep faith in the dark."

But her words proved a signal for worse to come. A tremor broke the stillness of the water before them. First ripples, then waves came running to the shore as if something huge below the surface were shuddering awake. They didn't have long to wait. Like the kraken from the deep, the Great Worm rose up with an eerie silence more terrifying than a blood-curdling scream.

The seven froze in their places as Crom Cruac looked down at them. He was blacker than the night itself, gargantuan and glittering like a spray of stars. A thousand eyes glared from his body for he had no head, no tail, no beginning or end. Each of the company felt the dreadful bane of that stare, eyes and eyes cutting through their being. He saw all, knew all.

And they sensed what he saw as he beheld them: seven specks of light besieged by darkness.

Where is the hostage?

Though he had no mouth to speak, his words reverberated in their minds. Stunned by his presence, by a reality they could barely conceive of, no one was able to answer at first.

Then Findabhair found the strength to speak. "I am here."

The others closed ranks around her.

Do you consent to be the sacrifice?

"She does not!" cried her friends.

The disturbance in Crom Cruac's thought shook the foundations of the night. The ground heaved beneath their feet. The dark sea began to boil. The distant mountains crumbled to dust as if a holocaust raged over the land.

YOU DARE TO BREAK A TIMELESS COVENANT.

They didn't wait for his attack but acted on instinct. Though none of them really knew how, they began to fight. Each went for the eyes, the only penetrable area. Spears pierced, swords hewed and arrows struck. Caught off guard by their audacity, the Worm was slow to retaliate. He lost a hundred eyes to Katie before he lunged down at her. With one sweeping gesture like the crack of a whip, he flung her upon the rocks. She crashed to the ground with a scream of pain. Mattie rushed to her side as the serpent turned to search out his next foe.

"My God, your leg is broken!"

"Prop me up in the rocks. He can't reach me there," Katie gasped through bleeding lips. "My arms are still good."

"You're wounded. You need—"

"There's no time for nursing!" she cried. "If we stop, all is lost."

Eyes wet with tears, Mattie did as she told him, wedging her battered body between two great stones.

"It takes more than one swipe to beat a redhead," she said, grimacing through her pain to comfort him. And once more the archer let fly her weapons.

When Mattie returned to the battle, he was enraged with a frenzy that sought revenge for Katie's wounds. Striking furiously at Crom Cruac, his lance was like a needle, pricking bubble after bubble.

Having learned their lesson from the blow to Katie, the others changed their tactics. With the quick movements of a macabre dance of death, they would attack and retreat to avoid the Worm. Now Crom Cruac came out of the lake, coiling upon the shore to crush them beneath his monstrous weight. But their smallness was an advantage, and they scattered in flight.

It was Dara who discovered the ultimate horror. After piercing a great eye, he didn't retreat fast enough. The viscous fluid splashed down on his arm and seared the flesh to the bone. Staggering back with a screech of agony, he warned the others. But the cry came too late.

Finvarra, the only one able to fly, had been striking from the air until he saw Findabhair in danger. She had been beaten to the ground, where she lay unmoving. The serpent was about to deal a fatal blow. Standing over her to bar the Worm's way, Finvarra plunged his spear into a cluster of eyes. The deadly rain oozed down upon him, setting his wings ablaze. Too shocked to cry out, he rolled into the water. When he crawled out again, the wondrous limbs trailed behind him like rags. His eyes were glazed with anguish. In his immortal life, he had never known pain.

"We must retreat!" cried Granny, who was using her staff like a sword. "To the rocks beside Katie!"

Mattie drew the serpent's attention to himself, even as Katie showered the air with the last of her arrows. Under this cover, the others withdrew. Granny and Dara carried Findabhair between them. Gwen led Finvarra, who swooned against her. At last all seven were crouched in the rocks.

A quiet fell over the desolate beach, broken only by the low moans of the wounded. Granny tore cloth from their garments to make bandages. All were bruised and burned, but some had injuries she knew she couldn't treat.

"He is dying," she said, staring into Finvarra's eyes. Then she laid her hand on Findabhair. "And so is she."

CHAPTER THIRTY-TWO

"No. This can't be happening," Gwen whispered.

Though she too was wounded, she accepted the pain as inevitable. It made sense after a fight. But not death.

Death made no sense at all.

Mattie stammered out his bewilderment.

"This doesn't . . . It isn't . . . It's not what I expected."

What had he expected? A glorious battle? A titanic struggle? Anything but this smell of burnt flesh, this distortion of limbs, these faces so tortured by suffering they were hardly recognizable. And worst of all, the cold fact of extinguished life. Was this what every soldier discovered when he went to war? That it's not a grand thing, not even a tragic one, only miserable and demeaning.

Katie stared sightlessly ahead of her, clenching her fists against the tides of pain. Would she die too in this dreary place? And for what reason would her life be cut off in its prime?

Gwen had gathered Findabhair into her arms. Her cousin was racked with the torment of internal wounds. Face streaked with tears, Gwen looked to Granny, who was holding Finvarra as he gasped for breath.

"Were we wrong after all? Is this our answer? Findabhair agreed to be the sacrifice and Finvarra with her. It can't be a coincidence that both of them will die."

"They may not be the only ones to die," Dara said suddenly. "Look!"

Out on the dark shore, the Great Worm lay motionless. Blood trickled over the sand from ragged holes where a multitude of eyes had been. A tremor of life was still in him, but it was as faint as a shadow. Slowly, painfully, he began to move, crawling toward the water as if to hide there. Then he disappeared beneath the surface without a sound.

"We have won," said Mattie. "Let us take our wounded home."

There was no joy of victory in the ragged band as they limped out from their shelter. The cost had been too high. Mattie cradled Findabhair in his arms. Katie leaned against Granny. Dara and Gwen supported Finvarra, who was fighting to stay conscious. Beyond them gleamed the Gates of Night. But before they could reach the shining portal, all froze with horror.

The waters of the tarn were moving. Ripples broke across the surface. Up rose Crom Cruac, fully healed and glistening.

Here was an Enemy who could not die.

It was too much to expect them to rally against a newly risen foe. Each knew in their hearts the situation was hopeless.

Do you surrender?

Wounded and broken, holding on to each other, the Company of Seven admitted defeat.

"What is your will?" Finvarra demanded, swaying on his feet.

As it has always been. Let the hostage yield to me.

Gwen clung to Findabhair. Katie cried out. Dara and Mattie stepped forward to offer themselves instead. Only Finvarra and Granny remained unmoved.

"Why?" asked Granny.

The Great Worm inclined his head toward her. All his eyes glittered like an infinity of stars. His aspect was neither good nor evil, but simply the cold disinterest of the universe itself.

Why life or why death?

Granny shook her head. "I accept the great mysteries as they stand. It's the particulars I question. Why you? Why this?"

Do you not know me, Wise Woman of Inch?

Something in his voice thrilled Granny to the very depths of her being.

I lie curled on the branch of the Tree of Life that bears

both Faërie and your world like twin golden apples. Two orbs,
two moons that eclipse each other, one fantasy, one reality, bal-
anced side by side. Humanity cannot exist without its
dreams, but for any dream to exist there must be a sacrifice.

A sigh issued from Granny's throat. She had
already decided to take Findabhair's place; now Crom
Cruac's words made it easier for her. Having lived her
life with myth and magic, she considered this a fitting
end.

No, Wise Woman, it is not you I take. Nor any of the
others who offer themselves. He knows who comes with me.
For the challenge of battle, I demand more than a human.
Only an immortal will satisfy me now.

Finvarra stepped forward without a word. He had
sensed the Worm's appetite and knew what it meant.
There was no time for farewells, no parting caresses for
friends or beloved. The darkness was gathering around
him. He had no choice but to go. Steadying himself
with the last gasp of his strength, wings tattered behind
him like a fallen angel's, he waded into the water alone.

Helplessly his six companions watched. Though
barely conscious, Findabhair suddenly understood.

A cry tore from her throat, high and wild with
grief. "Let me die with him!"

But like the night itself, the Worm was oblivious
to her pleas. As Crom Cruac sank beneath the waves,
so too did the ragged figure of the King of the Fairies.

CHAPTER THIRTY-THREE

How LONG THE SIX STOOD IN that netherworld of despair, they couldn't be certain. The change that took place was as slow and subtle as the arrival of dawn over the mountains. It was the absence of pain they noticed first. Their wounds had disappeared, leaving them fully restored. Then as the morning light unveiled the landscape, they saw where they were.

"We're on Inch," Dara managed to say, recognizing the shore of Lough Swilly and the lights of Rathmullan across the lake. "At the old fort."

All were utterly shaken. They were amazed to find themselves safe and back in their own world, yet the loss of their companion left no room for joy. It is difficult, indeed, to return home from the wars.

"The hostage yielded. The sacrifice was made."

Granny's voice echoed with sorrow. "The night of the Hunter's Moon has passed."

Findabhair's face was as pale and cold as marble. Only her eyes showed the intensity of her grief. Gently the others gathered around to offer their sympathy, but she was inconsolable.

Bowed down by sorrow, no one felt like talking. They walked from the fort onto the road that led to Granny's.

The full light of day was now bursting over the hills in all its splendour. Birds sang in the trees. The cry of a baby waking could be heard in a nearby house. They couldn't help but reflect that regardless of death, life still carried on.

It was when they reached the crossroads that they heard the sound. Music high and wild and tumultuously played. An impossible tune by a master fiddler.

And when they all came running, there he was, sitting on a large stone at the side of the road. Dressed in faded blue jeans and a white shirt with a red kerchief, he played his fiddle like a man without a care in the world. His face was nut-brown, as if weathered by sun and wind. His feet were bare. It was Finvarra, they had no doubt, yet he looked at them without recognition. When Findabhair drew near, he put down his instrument and smiled at her. Granny stepped forward.

"Dear King, are you well?"

"He seems to have lost his memory," said Findabhair.

"I know you are my friends," he said, then added

playfully, "and I think *you* are special to me, are you not?"

Findabhair didn't know whether to laugh or cry.

"Will you come with us?" Granny asked gently.

"Of course," he replied. "I have nowhere else to go."

The others exchanged glances at this remark. As they continued down the road, the King told his story.

"I beg your patience, friends, but this is all strange to me: the first day of my life that I hold in my memory. Who I am or where I come from, I do not know.

"Like a newborn babe I awoke, under a hawthorn bush, in a high place bordered by a sea of greenery. I was not alone, but surrounded by many creatures, birds and mice, foxes and hares. And people too. There was an old man with pointed ears, an old woman in a black shawl, and a tall red-haired lad accompanied by beautiful women. They were all weeping over me, and it was their cries that broke my sleep.

"'Why do you mourn on a day so filled with sunshine?' I asked them.

"Though none would answer my question, they led me to the place where you found me. I was told to stay there till six would come. You were my friends, they said, who would help me begin my new life. Then all lamented again before they took their leave of me.

"I pitied them greatly. To be so burdened with grief when the morning sang all around us. I kissed each warmly and bade them be glad. For life is too short for sorrow, is it not?"

But now Finvarra saw that his new companions also had tears in their eyes.

"Crom Cruac took his immortality," Gwen whispered to Katie.

"He's one of us now." She nodded back.

Though each felt the loss that had befallen the fairies, they could not help but be happy that he was alive. Findabhair's heart overflowed just looking at him, her beloved whom she thought she would never see again.

"You will explain this mystery to me, I hope?" Finvarra asked, regarding each in turn.

Six smiles shone through the tears as all agreed.

"A bit at a time, I think," Granny said. "For your own sake and the adjustments you will have to make."

"You are beginning the adventure of life as a man," Mattie told him.

"It's not so bad," Dara added with a grin.

"Do you recall anything?" Gwen asked.

Finvarra frowned as he regarded her. "Are you my love also?"

"No!" came the answer from three at once—Gwen, Dara and Findabhair.

With bursts of hilarity and lighter step, the Company of Seven strolled to Granny's. Findabhair and Finvarra drew closer together until they walked arm in arm. They looked no different a young couple than

Dara and Gwen, who were linked the same way. Though Mattie and Katie made plans to go home, the Seven knew they would meet up again and again. For the six "older" humans were well aware that a new life had been entrusted to their care.

And when the Company passed the Fargan Knowe, a wind suddenly gusted through the stand of trees. Leaves and small stones eddied in circles, rattling over the ground like the scamper of feet. A whisper sighed on the air.

The King passed by. Long live the King.